Illustrated **Timmi TOBBSON** Adventure

LEGACY OF THE INVENTOR

by J. I. WAGNER   Illustrated by J. G. RATTI

Written by J. I. Wagner.

Illustrated by J. G. Ratti.

Translated into English by Tracy Phua.

Book design © by freshamedia GmbH based on a layout from BookDesignTemplates.com.

Published by freshabooks.

Printed in the United States of America.

freshabooks is an imprint of:

freshamedia GmbH
Robert-Bosch-Str. 32
63303 Dreieich, Germany

www.timmitobbson.com

www.freshabooks.com

Hardcover: TBD
Paperback: ISBN 978-3-96326-772-7
E-Book: TBD

Printed in 2020.

Get the Fan-Package for FREE!

Go to TimmiTobbson.com to get your free downloads of the "**Police Interrogation Protocols**", "**The Art of Legacy**" as well as the "**Numbers Cheatbook**". (Available as PDF-files.)

Groups: Get a SIGNED Book Plate!

Should your school, book club or any other group order ten or more copies of *Legend of the Star Runner*, go ahead and write to me (at timmi@timmitobbson.com). Let me know how many copies were ordered, and I will send you just as many book plates (stickers that go inside the book) with my real (not printed) signature on them!

Get in Touch:
www.TimmiTobbson.com/im-a-fan
www.facebook.com/timmitobbson

That's just me.
Not much to say.

Timmi

For those who keep a twinkle in their eyes,

love in their hearts

and daydreams in their minds.

Lilli is one of my two best friends. She can be stubborn. And sassy. But above all, she is the bravest and boldest person I know.

She'd do anything to help a friend in need.

Lilli

The Chapters

Marvin is the other one of my two best friends. He loves animals. Whenever he gets excited, he bobs up and down on the spot. And he claps. It looks silly, but he doesn't care.

Marvin

Welcome to the World of Timmi Tobbson!

This is your adventure, first and foremost. Choose wisely to master each challenge. The magnifying glasses indicate what Timmi, Lilli and Marvin think about the difficulty of each puzzle.

Normal: Hard: Ultimate:

This is just their opinion. Maybe you will find a puzzle easy that they find hard or the other way around.

❖ ❖ ❖

You will find hints in the back of this book that can help you solve the upcoming picture mysteries.

❖ ❖ ❖

The solution to each puzzle is revealed in the subsequent chapter.

❖ ❖ ❖

You might find the following tools helpful, though they are not required to solve the puzzles:

Magnifying glass ❖ Pen ❖ Small mirror to read the hints section (mirror writing) ❖ Flashlight (for reading in the dark)

The Mysterious Symbol

Bang!

My bedroom door suddenly flew open, and all the stuff lying on the floor in front of it was swept back. To this day, I'm convinced some of my toys were pulverized between the door and the wall. Lilli stormed in. She seemed excited and was about to tell me something when the noise she'd caused made her stop in surprise and look around.

"Oops," she said with a sheepish smile, noticing the toys jammed behind the door. Without waiting for me to respond, she switched back to her previous state of intense excitement and said, "An adventure! We've got another adventure to go on!"

The loud bang had me sitting bolt upright in bed and staring at Lilli dumbfounded.

"You're still in your pajamas," she said, surprised.

"It's summer break. My favorite author's new book is out, and this morning I just—"

"Got it. Get dressed," Lilli interrupted.

"—started reading it."

"Marvin's waiting!"

"Marvin's waiting?"

"Yep. We have to go."

For a moment, I was speechless. "Would you go out for a minute then?" I asked finally.

"Um, no," she replied.

"So I can get dressed."

"I'll look away, okay?" said Lilli and briskly turned on her left heel so her back was to me. "Then I can tell you about this while you do." She held up a newspaper.

"What about it?" I asked.

"Today, all the big daily papers published a massive, full-page ad for a treasure hunt!"

"Let me see that," I said. Getting dressed could wait. This I had to see now.

"I knew it," she said, turning swiftly back around, coming over to my bed and spreading the newspaper out on the covers. "Take a look at that," she said with a mischievous grin.

A mysterious illustration took up almost the whole page. Above it, were the words *Find Me!*

A short text was printed in each of three white circles. I read the first out quietly:

> *Go into my world and search, my friend.*
> *The treasure map is there on the end.*

"So there's a treasure map hidden somewhere," I mused.

"Looks like it. Keep reading," said Lilli impatiently.

My eyes wandered to the lines in the second circle, which I read out quietly too:

> *The elixir is ready; it must see the light of day.*
> *But the Guardians plan to hide it away.*

I stared in disbelief at the text. "No way," I said. "An elixir. The Guardians. Do you think this has something to do with our last adventure?"

Not too long ago, we'd discovered a mysterious, ancient book which apparently contained important, secret knowledge. Unfortunately, we'd never gotten to read it, because we'd only just discovered it when it was taken from us by a sinister secret order called the *Guardians of the Dark Power*.

Then the book had disappeared without a trace. We only knew its title. Translated, it meant *Elixir*.

"Yeah, of course, sleepyhead."

"I only just woke up. It's normal to be a bit dozy."

"Yeah right. You've been awake for ages."

"What makes you say that?"

"Well, you told me what you've been doing this morning, and looking closely I can tell you've been doing it for quite some time."

Why did Lilli think I must have been awake longer than just a few minutes?

The solution to each puzzle is revealed at the beginning of the following chapter. You can find hints at the back of this book.

Into My World

I'd told Lilli I'd started reading my favorite author's new book that morning. However, I'd almost devoured half of it already. She could tell because I was holding the book open to the page I was up to. So she had every reason to believe I'd been awake a long time already.

"Okay, what else does it say?" I asked and read out the third and final section:

The elixir breaks down tomorrow, 10 p.m.
Unless you manage to save it by then.

"Apparently we only have till ten tomorrow night to solve the puzzle," I said.

"Yeah, sounds like something's going to happen after that. Now have a look at this." Lilli pointed to the two letters on the right below the box. "J.E. must stand for James Eckles. Ever heard of him? He's a famous archeologist. But most of all, he's considered one of the greatest inventors of our time. Or he was. He's missing."

"Missing?" I asked.

"Without a trace. For a few weeks now," said Lilli.

"Without a trace? How did he put the ad in the newspaper then?" I wondered quietly.

"Maybe he arranged it before his disappearance. I'll tell you the rest when we get to the museum," she said, jumping to her feet. "Don't forget your walkie-talkie."

"The museum?" I asked.

"I'll wait for you downstairs," replied Lilli with a grin and bounced out of the room.

I quickly got dressed and grabbed my adventure bag. I'd put it together for just this kind of situation. It contained my own handwritten Adventurers and Detectives' Handbook, fingerprint powder, a magnifying glass and more. And of course a walkie-talkie.

❖ ❖ ❖

A short while later, we entered the majestic-looking Museum of Technology. Marvin was waiting for us inside where it was cool.

"Hey, how's it going?" I asked quietly.

He was clutching his sketch pad, which he always had on him lately and bobbing up and down on the balls of his feet. "Do you think this is going to be the start of another adventure?" he asked eagerly, eyes wide.

"I think the adventure has already begun," I whispered.

Lilli smiled at us. "Look Timmi," she said, pointing to a sign. It read: *The World of James Eckles.*

She held her newspaper up again. *"Go into my world and search, my friend. The treasure map is there on the end,"* she read out loud, pointing to the circle with the cryptic clue. "We've found his *world.* Do you get it, Timmi? *Go into my world.* It means this exhibit. So the treasure map must be on the end of something in here."

"But the end of what?" asked Marvin excitedly. "I've already looked all over and couldn't find anything." For a moment, he looked dejected. "Then I drew pictures of all the museum visitors," he went on more enthusiastically.

"Why would you do that?" I asked.

"Because we're hardly going to be the only ones going after the treasure," he replied, his eyes growing wide. "If someone else finds the treasure map before we do, they might steal it. This way, at least we've got a sketch of the thief."

"Okay, if you say so," I said and scanned the room. It was stuffed full of all kinds of bizarre-looking gadgets, sculptures and even a life-sized model of the inventor James Eckles himself. In the center stood a strange machine with a digital countdown on a glass pane. I had to get a closer look at that.

But then things took an unexpected turn.

Suddenly, a loud alarm went off, giving us an awful fright. In an instant, metallic shutters came down over all the windows. A heavy metal plate even closed over the glass dome in the roof, shutting out all daylight within a few seconds. You couldn't see a thing anymore.

Then the alarm fell silent, and everything went eerily quiet. The occasional murmurs of nervous visitors echoed through the rooms. Every so often you could hear footsteps.

"The thief is already here," Marvin whispered.

We huddled tightly together, not moving. When the emergency lighting finally came on, and we could see again, Marvin said, "Something's different."

What had changed apart from the lighting?

The Five Suspects

Marvin had spent the entire morning in this room and noticed right away that the flag had disappeared from the staff in the hand of the life-sized statue of the inventor. So that was what the line *there on the end* meant. The treasure map must have been printed on the flag.

The museum employees reassured the visitors, but no-one was allowed to leave the building. Everyone had to assemble in the lobby. We eyed the other visitors suspiciously because one of them had to be the thief.

"Please accept our sincerest apologies," said one of the museum employees. "My name is Mr. Baker. I'm responsible for security in the museum. The alarm appears to have been activated because a crown was moved from its proper location. It wasn't stolen, however; we found it somewhere else. Still, this is a serious matter. Did any of you see anything? Any information is most welcome."

"Hasn't anyone noticed the flag was stolen?" Lilli whispered.

"We should tell them then," said Marvin.

"No, no, no," hissed Lilli.

"Young lady, is there something you'd like to say?" asked Mr. Baker, striding over to us and drawing himself up in front of Lilli. He was an old, bearded man with gray hair and a dark-blue uniform with golden buttons. He put his hands on his hips and considered Lilli suspiciously, although far from pulling off terrifying, he rather resembled a cuddly bear.

"Me? No."

"Well, if you have something to say, say it now. The police will be here soon."

"Is it possible something was actually stolen?"

"No, I don't think so. Why do you ask?"

"How does the alarm work?"

"You can only turn it off with one of these keycards," said Mr. Baker, proudly showing us the red card dangling from his lanyard.

"Cool," said Lilli. "But that's not what I meant. Once the alarm has been activated, someone could steal a second object. That wouldn't activate a second alarm, right?"

"Hmm, no. There's only one alarm," he said and scratched his beard. "But all the pieces are protected by electronic sensors. We'd notice if something were missing."

"What about if someone only wanted to steal a certain part of an exhibit piece?"

"Okay, that might be possible. But who'd want to do that?" he asked with a smile.

"Yeah, who'd want to do that?" repeated Lilli, grinning.

"Yes, exactly," laughed the museum employee before clapping his hands together and turning back to the other visitors. "Right, where were we? Well, whatever the case, thank you for your patience everyone. The police will be here soon. They'll take down your details, but since nothing was actually stolen, I think you'll be able to leave then."

"Why didn't you tell him?" I whispered.

"One of the visitors has the flag, which is probably the treasure map," said Lilli. "Shouldn't we find out who the thief is and what he or she is up to?"

"You mean we're going to follow them?" asked Marvin and clapped his hands excitedly.

"But which one is our thief?" I asked.

"I don't have a clue," Lilli admitted, eyeing up the visitors.

"Let's see the sketches you did of the visitors again, Marvin," I suggested. "Maybe we'll find a clue."

Marvin held up his sketch pad. For the past few months, you never saw him without his pad and pencil. All that practice was paying off. Because Marvin loved animals so much, he mostly drew them, but he seemed to have a knack for people too.

"Wow, they're great, Marvin," I said.

"Good job, Marvin," Lilli agreed.

He gave us a bashful smile. We discreetly compared the drawings to the people present.

"Hey, look at this," Lilli whispered and pointed to one of the drawings.

 What did Lilli notice?

The Thief

Marvin did all his drawings before the alarm went off. At that time, the man with the hat and walking stick was still in possession of a polka-dot bag. When we looked at the old man now, we noticed he no longer had the bag. Rather it now lay in the storage basket of the stroller a young mother was rocking back and forth.

So we assumed the man with the hat and walking stick must be the culprit. We assigned him the codename "the Hat".

According to our theory, "the Hat" must have stolen the flag and put it in his polka-dot bag. Then he placed said bag in the stroller, planning to have the mother smuggle the stolen property out of the museum, because if they did search the stroller no-one would possibly suspect him. Later he would probably steal the bag back from the unsuspecting lady.

We decided to follow the Hat. As soon as he recovered the bag, we'd call the police. Then they'd catch him red-handed.

So when the police arrived at the museum, we decided not to mention our suspicions yet. The mother with the baby was allowed to leave the museum soon afterwards, once she'd been questioned and her details had been taken down.

"We can't lose her," whispered Lilli.

We waited nervously for our turn to be questioned, which we got through swiftly by answering every question quick as a shot. A short while later, a police officer escorted us to the exit, but the Hat was allowed to leave at exactly the same time. When he caught up to us, I noticed a tattoo on the back of his hand.

"You try to find the mom with the stroller. I'll shadow the Hat," I said in a whisper so my target couldn't hear. "Turn on your walkie-talkies."

We discreetly pulled out our walkie-talkies and switched them on.

When the museum doors opened, the blazing midday heat beat down on us. We were greeted by an absolutely chaotic crowd of people: The sprawling marketplace was in the middle of its noon rush.

The Hat, who clearly didn't even need his walking stick, suddenly darted down the steps full throttle and plunged into the thronging masses of the marketplace. I hadn't been expecting that. It took me a moment to react before I took up the chase, but by then I'd already lost sight of him. I couldn't let the Hat get away. Lilli and Marvin's mission was to find the mother, the baby and above all the bag containing the flag hidden inside the stroller. They too raced down the stairs.

The police officer who had escorted us to the exit stared after us, shaking his head in amazement.

Only a few feet into the crowded marketplace, I began to lose hope. There was no sign of the Hat. I looked around in panic.

"I've lost him," I said into my walkie-talkie.

"There's a tower at the end of the square," Marvin replied. "At the top, there's a café with a balcony."

"We'll have an awesome view from up there," I said.

"Okay, meet you there," said Lilli. "I brought my binoculars."

The café was a posh establishment. When we entered the lobby, we automatically slowed our steps. The classical music, the waiters with bowties and the interior styling reminiscent of an old royal palace seemed to somehow subdue us. But not for long.

Lilli caught sight of a stone spiral staircase with a red carpet runner and dashed up it. Moments later we found ourselves on the narrow balcony attracting many a skeptical look. Lilli didn't seem bothered by it; she was already scanning the marketplace with her binoculars.

"There she is! I see her," Lilli cried out happily.

"The mom with the stroller? Where?" I asked.

"Hang on. She doesn't have the bag anymore."

"No way," I murmured.

"Yep. It's gone," Lilli said and held the binoculars out to us.

Marvin grabbed them and had a look.

"Which table are you with?" a waiter now asked us.

Lilli and I exchanged a brief but significant look.

"If you're not with one of the tables, I'm going to have to ask you to leave."

"I think I see the bag," cried Marvin excitedly, which had all the guests looking over at us.

"Where?" asked Lilli.

"You need to leave now," the waiter said, placing a hand on Marvin's upper arm.

"A piece of strawberry cheesecake," Marvin yelled and shook the hand off.

"That will be twelve dollars," the waiter warned him, rolling his eyes.

"He's changed his clothes," yelled Marvin, "but that's the Hat. Definitely. He has the bag!"

Can you find the man codenamed "the Hat"?

The Chase

"Okay, the Hat's standing at the crosswalk opposite the post office. He has the bag," said Marvin.

A few guests chuckled and shook their heads.

"The hat's standing at the crosswalk opposite the post office," one of them repeated in amusement.

"He's got his coat on inside out, same with his hat. Now they're all purple. He's taken off the white beard and wig too. They're sticking out of the pocket of his jacket," said Marvin.

Quick as a flash, Lilli rushed back into the café and down the stairs. I followed. Marvin had to stay there and keep an eye on our target till Lilli and I caught up with him. That meant he had to stall the waiter. He gathered up all his courage and imagined what Lilli would say in this situation.

"Twelve bucks for a piece of strawberry cheesecake?" he asked incredulously.

The waiter pointed to the stairs. "You're going to lose your friends."

Yes, Marvin would have desperately loved to run after us. Instead, he said, "You never lose anyone with these. They're called binoculars." He waved them around in front of the waiter. "Ever heard of them?"

The waiter gave Marvin a silent glare as if warning him not to get sassy on top of everything else.

"They make your vision as sharp as a hawk's. Even mine," said Marvin and peered once more through the binoculars. The Hat hadn't moved from the spot. Now Marvin could also see Lilli and me, pushing our way through the crowd. "See? A piece of strawberry cheesecake only costs three bucks down there," Marvin yelled at the waiter. "Three!"

◆ ◆ ◆

I was having trouble keeping up with Lilli. She scurried between people with a great deal of agility and assertiveness. "Marvin, is he still there?" I asked, wheezing into the walkie-talkie.

"I'm afraid so. Here, I'll put him on," he said to my surprise. A few seconds of silence followed. "He doesn't want to talk to you."

"Not the waiter, the Hat, Marvin!"

"Oh, right. Yep, he's still there. Hang on, the light's turning green. He's on the move."

Lilli and I now came to a tightly packed row of stalls which blocked off the direct route to the crosswalk.

"Left or right?" Lilli asked Marvin through the walkie-talkie.

"Let me go," came a screech through our units. Then we heard Marvin call out to the café guests, "I'm an artist! Who wants their portrait drawn?"

"Left or right?" Lilli repeated impatiently.

"Right! Go around to the right!" Marvin finally answered.

We dashed off.

"There's a gap between two stalls on your left. Go through it!" he instructed.

We located the shortcut, squeezed through and found ourselves by the crosswalk. The light was just turning back to red.

"Unbelievable," Lilli grumbled as the tightly packed cars and trucks before us began to move. I peered desperately through the traffic, hoping to catch a glimpse of the Hat on the other side of the street.

"Marvin? Can you see him?" I asked into my walkie-talkie.

"Yeah, he's running down the street. Now he's turning down the first little lane on the left," Marvin told us. "And now I can't see him anymore."

Like two tigers in a cage, Lilli and I paced back and forth, our eyes fixed on the red crosswalk light. When it finally turned green, we took off. First down the street opposite and then left down the little lane.

The city noise ebbed away, and the tall building walls cast a cool shadow. They extended along both sides of the lane, with doors leading into stairwells and apartments. A glance upward revealed balconies, some of which were used to dry laundry and some of which were used as comfy relaxation retreats. At the other end of the lane before us, you could see traffic again, driving by in the bright sunlight.

There was no sign of our target.

"We've lost him. I don't believe it," Lilli yelled in annoyance.

"Wait," I told Lilli. "I think he's gone into one of the buildings."

 Why did I think the suspect had gone into one of the buildings? And which one was it?

The Thieves' Den

All around the puddle of laundry water, you could see footprints. Whoever made them must have stepped in the puddle not long ago. Beside one of the sets of footprints, you could make out little round spots, probably from a walking stick. The Hat had entered the stairwell behind the blue door.

"The windows on the third-floor balcony are covered with newspaper," I whispered.

"Someone doesn't want anyone looking into the apartment," said Lilli.

I spoke into my walkie-talkie. "Marvin? We've found the Hat's apartment. We're going to get the police now."

"Okay," came the crackly reply. "I just have to quickly finish drawing someone."

❖ ❖ ❖

A short while later, Marvin had joined us again, and we stood with two police officers outside the apartment door on the third story, behind which we guessed the Hat's hideout was to be found. You could hear noises through the door. We watched eagerly as one of the officers knocked.

"Hello? This is Inspector Hallewell," she called.

Instantly the noises behind the door became hectic. It sounded as if someone were feverishly packing things up. Something banged. Then it went quiet as a mouse.

"Hello?" called the inspector again. "Open up, please."

Lilli hurried to the stairwell window overlooking the little alleyway. She opened it and peered out. "He's on the balcony. He's escaping!"

"Unbelievable," yelled Inspector Hallewell. "Stay here."

Quick as a flash, the officers ran down the stairs and took up pursuit. Out the window, we saw them running down the lane after the suspect.

"What now?" I sighed once they were out of sight.

"Twelve-dollar strawberry cheesecake?" offered Marvin and held the delicious snack under our noses.

We laughed, sitting down by the apartment door to enjoy the sweet treat. Marvin told us how he'd gotten it from a kind customer in exchange for a portrait.

Suddenly, the door to the thieves' den opened.

We sat frozen. One after the other, five men, all of them muscular and with the aura of a military strike force, marched out of the apartment and down the stairs as if it were the most natural thing in the world. Their movements were swift but not hectic, and they carried all kinds of boxes and backpacks. Faces frozen in shock, jaws hanging open, we stared after them. They didn't pay us any attention. The last one let the door fall closed behind him. Almost, at least, because I discreetly took Marvin's drawing pencil, which lay next to him on the ground, and jammed it in the rapidly closing gap. The man didn't seem to miss the sound of the door falling shut. The group's footsteps echoed through the stairwell.

"Who were *they*?" asked Lilli.

"Dunno, but I don't want to go after them," Marvin murmured.

"So escaping off the balcony was just a distraction," I whispered. Standing, I dusted myself off and crept over to the open window. The men were leaving the building and heading down the lane, one after the other.

When the last one appeared below, he called out to the person in front of him, "You've got the street map, right?"

"No, not me," the man replied without turning back or slowing his pace.

The last gangster stopped where he was and patted his pockets. Lilli appeared beside me at the window.

"I think they forgot something. A map," I whispered to her.

"Hurry," said Lilli. She spun around and dashed into the apartment.

Marvin and I exchanged a look.

"It's always the same with her," he said, gulping down the last bite of cheesecake and clambering to his feet.

I gazed back down into the alley. There, the guy bringing up the rear was now checking his backpack as the others got farther and farther ahead.

"Help Lilli find the street map. He'll be back up in a minute," I told Marvin. But he was already in the apartment with Lilli.

With growing panic, I watched as moments later the gangster shouldered his pack, ready to come back up.

"We've got company," I yelled to the others.

"It's a total mess in here," I heard Lilli shout back.

Now the man entered the stairwell below us.

I rushed into the apartment. In the thieves' den, chaos reigned.

"Now or never," I whispered.

"We can't find anything," said Marvin, sounding desperate.

Below I heard the gangster hastily climbing the steps.

"Let's get out of here then!" I yelled.

"I've got it," said Lilli.

Where was the street map?

The Hidden Face

A quick look at the street map she'd found behind the old gramophone was all Lilli needed. She memorized what she saw.

But now it was too late to leave the apartment. The gangster was already trudging up the steps to our floor.

As quickly and quietly as I could, I closed the apartment door. Lilli placed the map in a conspicuous position right in the middle of the room so the thief would find it as soon as he walked in.

Then we hurried into the bedroom to hide.

We heard the door opening and the man storming inside. He promptly stopped short, murmured something to himself and immediately turned back around. Moments later the apartment door closed.

It turned out he had found the map, because when we left our hiding place it was gone. Then we continued to search the thieves' den while we waited for the police to get back, but we didn't find any additional clues. When the officers finally did return to the apartment, they didn't have any good news either. Unfortunately they had lost sight of the Hat in the confusion of the marketplace. They took us back to the police station to get our statements.

◆ ◆ ◆

"And you're sure the map showed Bloodhound Castle?" asked Inspector Hallewell for about the hundredth time.

"Absolutely certain," Lilli grumbled, exhausted.

The police station was like an oven. Outside it was hot, but at least a pleasant breeze was blowing. Inside the air was still, and everyone was sweating. We'd convinced the inspector to send a squad car to Bloodhound Castle because we assumed the gang would soon strike there. The officers had taken up their position over an hour ago.

Meanwhile Inspector Hallewell had found out quite a bit about Bloodhound Castle. It was the ruins of an old fortress located in the middle of a swamp. It owed its name to a legend which told of massive wild dogs that supposedly roamed the region. Inspector Hallewell considered it to be nothing more than a myth designed to keep strangers away from the castle and the very dangerous swamplands.

The biggest surprise her research had revealed, however, was the fact that Bloodhound Castle had been bought by James Eckles a few years earlier. The same James Eckles who was behind the treasure hunt we'd been on since this morning. That could hardly be a coincidence. The flag stolen from the museum must have contained a clue pointing to Bloodhound Castle. That would have been why the gang had marked the old ruins on the map and were probably on their way there by now.

"Radio the squad car again," the inspector said to a colleague who sat at a large piece of equipment covered in all kinds of buttons and gauges. The latter sighed and turned a knob till the frequency 103.02 appeared on a display.

"Second precinct here. How's it looking, team?" she spoke into a microphone.

"This is squad car five. No sign of movement. How long are we supposed to sit around here waiting?" came the crackly response through the loudspeaker.

Inspector Hallewell took a deep breath and eyed us carefully. "Tell him to hang in there another two hours," she told her colleague who passed on the order.

A young police officer rushed over to us waving a large manila envelope. "Here are the photos from the security camera," he called.

"From the museum? Put them on the table!" ordered the inspector, and we all gathered around to examine them.

The images were all of the Hat. The Hat entering the museum, the Hat sauntering through the exhibit, the Hat picking up the crown to set off the alarm, the Hat shoving the flag in his bag and finally the Hat placing the bag into the stroller.

"I just don't believe it," said the inspector.

"What is it?" asked the young officer.

"You can't see his face in any of the photos. Thanks to you kids, we know about the tattoo on the back of his hand, but a shot of his face would be really helpful."

We all took another close look at the pictures.

"You're right," I said.

"He knew where the security cameras were," the inspector mused.

"And cleverly used his hat as cover," her colleague added.

"We may have a description of his appearance from various people, yourselves included, but that's no substitute for a real photo," Inspector Hallewell said, looking at us. "There's not a single shot of his face."

"Are you sure about that?" asked Marvin to the astonishment of all.

 Why did Marvin think there may have been a photo of the Hat's face after all?

The Ghost Rail

If the museum guard really did take a photo of the woman with the baby right when the Hat was walking across the background, then his face must have been visible in it too. We said goodbye to the inspector who was confident she could get hold of the photos on the camera.

But Lilli wasn't even thinking about going home. She insisted on heading over to Bloodhound Castle. "It's only an hour by foot if we walk across country," she said. "I know the way. Besides, the cops are already there. They can bring us back afterwards."

In short: there was no dissuading her.

❖ ❖ ❖

By now it was late afternoon, and the sun still burned mercilessly down on us as we set off for Bloodhound Castle. We followed the tracks of an old, out-of-service railway line which had long since been swallowed up by the plant life growing unchecked around it. At first the tracks led us through fields and meadows, but with time the landscape changed, getting swampier and swampier. What's more, we weren't progressing nearly as quickly as we'd expected. Mostly thanks to Marvin, who was constantly discovering new animals he just had to sketch. Eventually we managed to convince him we were running out of time and for now he better not give in to his urge to draw. From then on, my best friend plodded forlornly along behind us.

"In the newspaper ad, the one announcing the treasure hunt, James Eckles mentioned an elixir," he said. "What do you think the elixir does?"

"It must be something really important," said Lilli. "Why else would James Eckles, the greatest inventor in the world, bother with it? Why would a genius like that disappear without a trace and then go to all that trouble to set up a treasure hunt from wherever he's hiding? Why would a gang of professional thieves be after the elixir?"

"Maybe it gives you superpowers. Maybe it lets you stop time. Or talk to animals. Or move things with your mind," Marvin chattered away.

Meanwhile I couldn't help thinking of the Guardians of the Dark Power again. The text had to have been referring to them when it said *But the Guardians plan to hide it away.* During our last adventure, we'd already had an unfortunate run-in with this powerful secret organization.

In my mind's eye, I saw the ancient book we'd found back then. It had been bound in brown leather with a red border. According to the title, it had been about an elixir too. We never found out more because the Guardians had immediately taken the book away from us. Had we been on the trail of the same secret back then as we were today?

"I think it'll be something that helps humankind," said Lilli.

"Like chocolate?" asked Marvin.

"Something more important," she said.

"Like chocolate ice cream!" he cried out with conviction.

"I wouldn't say no to one of those right now," sighed Lilli.

"Do you think the Guardians of the Dark Power threatened James Eckles and forced him to go into hiding?" I asked. "Maybe because he managed to make the elixir?"

"Yeah, that could well be," said Lilli. "The Guardians want to protect the secret of the elixir."

The covert organization was not only powerful but also creepy. According to legend, you could tell a Guardian by their eyes and mouth. Where those should have been, their faces had nothing but pitch-black darkness. Despite the heat, a shiver ran down my spine.

We plodded along the old train tracks in silence for a while, until Lilli suddenly stopped short and gaped at the ground in front of her feet.

"Excuse me, but what on earth is *that*?" she asked.

We peered over her shoulder and stared at the imprint of a massive dog's paw. Because of the moisture from the swamplands nearby, the ground here was still muddy despite the heat. The impression looked fresh. Was the legend of the roaming bloodhounds perhaps true after all?

"Just because an animal has big feet doesn't mean it's dangerous," whispered Marvin. "Your feet are big too, Lilli."

Normally this would have earned Marvin a sassy retort from Lilli, but she was staring down, transfixed, as she stuck her right foot into the impression. There was plenty of room for her whole shoe.

"Not as big as this animal's," Lilli whispered nervously.

Suddenly a rustling sound came from somewhere behind us. I don't remember who was first to be overcome by panic, but in the end, we were all running like crazy along the tracks. Just before we got too puffed to go on, we saw a kind of illegal garbage dump beside the tracks.

"Quick, let's find a place to hide," I suggested.

 Where did we hide?

The Eerie Village

We hid in the big cart which sank noticeably with our additional weight. After braving the heat under the tarp a few minutes, everything was still quiet, so we gathered up our courage and continued on our journey.

We'd now been on the road much longer than Lilli had originally thought we would. The sun shone relentlessly on our faces, although it was now low in the sky and not as powerful as before. We doggedly continued to follow the abandoned tracks because we knew they would lead us to the little village that lay just before Bloodhound Castle.

However, we didn't arrive until after night had fallen.

The moon shone brightly, and passing clouds cast eerie shadows on the few antiquated-looking cottages in the village. Almost all the buildings lay in darkness and looked deserted. Only the windows of an inn were lit up.

"It's kind of creepy here," whispered Marvin.

"Maybe we can call our parents in there," I said, gesturing to the inn. "We can't cross the swamp in the dark, anyway. And since we can't go any farther, they could come get us."

Stepping through the creaky wooden door of the inn, we found ourselves in a little lounge. Behind the short bar stood a grim-looking elderly lady cleaning glasses. At one of the three round tables sat two equally grouchy-looking men drinking out of large goblets. They all stared at us in astonishment. For a few seconds, no-one said a word. The quiet ticking of a clock was the only sound.

"What in the world are you kids doing here?" the landlady finally growled.

"I'll wait outside then," whispered Marvin and got an elbow in the ribs from Lilli.

"We're lost," I said. "We'd like to call our parents."

The landlady stuck a toothpick in her mouth, chewed on it and eyed us quietly. Had I said something stupid?

"We want them to come get us," I added.

"What in the world are you doing here?" repeated the landlady gruffly.

One of the men at the table murmured something unintelligible. The other nodded.

"We want to go to Bloodhound Castle," said Lilli.

At the mention of that name, the woman and her two guests positively froze. They looked petrified. All three stared at us, speechless. I was gradually starting to feel uneasy too.

A child's voice broke the silence. "I could take you."

"Who asked you?" shouted the landlady. "Get to your room!"

A girl around our age slunk out of a dark alcove, ran behind the bar and in seconds had disappeared again.

"You're not going anywhere," said the landlady. "Don't you know about the bloodhounds?"

"Those are just fairytales," said Lilli.

The landlady stared at her aghast. Out of nowhere, she slammed her fist down on the bar. "It's people who talk that way they get first," she hissed.

We flinched.

"I really don't like it here," whispered Marvin.

"Could we use the phone?" I asked, hoping to change the subject.

"There's no phone here," she said and shrugged. "Besides, you can only drive as far as Bloodhound Castle. Then you have to go through the swamp to get here. Your parents would have no way of reaching you. You'll stay here tonight. Tomorrow morning we'll decide what to do."

Lilli and Marvin gave me questioning looks. Was she telling the truth? Should we make a run for it? Or stay the night? I gave a little nod to say we better accept the offer.

❖ ❖ ❖

A short while later, we found ourselves in a modest yet comfortable guest room on the top floor. The landlady put a carafe of water, some potato soup and bread in the room for us and slammed the wooden door shut behind her.

Then we heard her turn the key.

Lilli tugged on the door handle and shook the door. "I don't believe it. She locked us in," she said, running to the window and pulling the curtains open.

A row of thick metal bars stared calmly back at us. We wouldn't be getting out that way. Lilli leaned against the wall and slid slowly to the floor. I sat down beside her. Being locked in wouldn't do. We had to get out of here.

Marvin peered through the keyhole. "Thought so," he said happily. "She left the key in the lock."

Without wasting another word, he went to the little table and dug into the warm potato soup.

I cleared my throat, and he noticed our puzzled expressions.

"Why are you looking at me like that? You realize we can get out of here anytime we want, right?" He gave us a satisfied grin and continued slurping his soup.

Making as little noise as possible, how could we have gotten hold of the key which was stuck in the door from the outside in order to open it?

Light in the Darkness

We waited till the inn went quiet. The landlady was surely in bed by now. Then we shoved the towel that had been hanging over the radiator a decent way through the gap under the door. It now covered the ground beneath the keyhole on the other side. Next we pushed the key out of the lock with the help of one of the sticks we'd found in the fragrance diffuser on the desk. It fell onto the fabric without a sound, and we pulled the towel, along with the key, back through the crack into the room.

Now we could unlock the door.

First we turned off the light and slipped out of our shoes to walk as quietly as possible. Then we slowly unlocked and opened it. For a moment, we paused and listened. Everything remained quiet.

Carefully we crept down the stairs and reached the lounge. We approached the exit on tiptoes.

Suddenly, I thought I heard a noise in the darkness behind us. I held my arm up, and we all froze.

"Do you still want to go to Bloodhound Castle?" asked a girl's voice quietly. "I can take you."

Relieved, we turned to face her.

"That would be fantastic," whispered Lilli.

❖ ❖ ❖

A few minutes later, we found ourselves in the middle of a swampy landscape. The girl, whose name was Amy, went ahead of us, lighting up the darkness with a lantern. We really needed it, because the moon hung behind a curtain of clouds and barely gave off any light. What's more, a veil of fog lay all around us.

Amy said we should try to step exactly where she did, because you really couldn't make out any proper path, and one false step could see us sinking into the swamp.

"We've got a flashlight," murmured Marvin.

"It'll just attract the dogs," said Amy. "They recognize my lantern. They leave me alone."

"Don't say the story about the dogs is true?" asked Marvin.

"Sure is. I've seen them with my own eyes plenty of times. They're black," she said and shone the light of her lantern in Marvin's face. "Their eyes glow red in the dark. I'm sure they're not from this world."

"Not from this world?" asked Marvin in awe.

"There must be a portal to another dimension somewhere in the swamp. I've tried looking for it but haven't found anything yet."

A short distance off, I saw lights. They looked like windows.

"Is that Bloodhound Castle over there?" I asked.

Amy lowered her lantern and looked in the direction I was pointing. "Yeah. But no-one lives in the castle at the moment. Why are there lights on?"

When we got closer, the mist around us thinned. We could make out three cars parked near the main entrance. There wasn't a soul in sight. Amy extinguished her lantern, and we crept over to within a few feet of one of the cars by the light of the moon. Here we said goodbye to Amy, who was clearly unnerved by these unfamiliar visitors.

Then we darted between the cars, across the castle courtyard and hid behind a column. From here we had a decent view of everything happening at the entrance to Bloodhound Castle.

"What do we do now?" asked Lilli.

Suddenly, headlights shone on her face. Startled, we pressed ourselves hard up against the wall so we were hidden in the shadows. A small truck approached, then parked behind the other vehicles. The next moment, the main door to the castle opened. Light poured over the pebbles in the courtyard, and two men stepped outside. They were tall and muscular. Both wore strange vests with all kinds of pockets, and one had a professional walkie-talkie clipped to the waistband of his pants, the glowing numbers clearly indicating the frequency at which it was set. Only now did my gaze fall on the other pieces of equipment standing in the driveway next to the vehicles. Whoever these people were, they knew what they were doing.

"Are those the thieves from the apartment?" asked Lilli.

"It must be them," I said. "I think the guy on the left is the Hat."

"But he doesn't look old and frail at all," said Marvin.

Before I could answer, Lilli whispered excitedly, "Remember the police car Inspector Hallewell sent to wait for the gang here at the castle?"

"Sure," I said. "They'll be long gone by now. What about them?"

"They never had a hope of catching them," replied Lilli. "The thieves knew full well they were waiting for them here."

"Hang on a sec. What makes you say that?" asked Marvin.

How could I tell the man on the left was the Hat?

Why did Lilli think the police never had a hope of catching the gang?

BONUS QUESTION

Bloodhound Castle

Back in the museum, I had already noticed the bump in the Hat's nose, and the gangster on the left had the same unusual shape to his. But above all, they both had the same distinctive tattoo on the backs of their hands. In the museum, the Hat had only been pretending he was old. His hair and his feeble appearance had been nothing but a disguise. In reality, he was swift and strong, as we'd seen when he had escaped off the balcony. To me, there was no question. This man was clearly the Hat.

Lilli had noticed the walkie-talkie on the Hat's waistband. It was set to 103.02. We'd heard of this wavelength before, a few hours earlier at the police station. Inspector Hallewell used it to communicate with the patrol car staking out Bloodhound Castle. So the gang of thieves had been listening to that same frequency and knew not to approach the castle until the coast was clear.

The Hat seemed to be the leader of the gang. He ordered the driver and the other thug to pull something off the truck's cargo bed. Right now no-one was looking in our direction.

"Wait here," I whispered, dashing around the column and over to the front door. Cautiously I peered inside the castle. There was a spacious lobby with antique furniture and all kinds of equipment which must have belonged to the gang.

Then I saw it. The flag lay spread out on a small collapsible table.

My heart pounded frantically. Now or never. I ducked down to avoid being seen as I slipped through the front door, snatched up the flag and dashed back out to the others.

"I've got it. Let's get out of here!" I said. "Follow the wall."

A few minutes later, we examined our prize by the light of the moon.

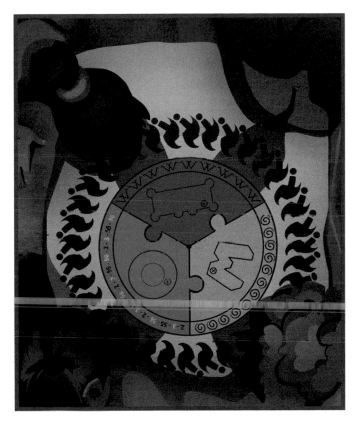

"The picture on the purple part could just about be the outline of Bloodhound Castle," whispered Lilli. "The round bits are the towers. Then maybe the X marks where something is hidden."

"Yeah, makes sense," I said. "No idea what the other pictures are meant to be though. Do you think they're also outlines of buildings? And what do the symbols on the borders of the puzzle pieces mean?"

"One thing at a time. *Now* we have to go *there*," said Marvin and pointed to the *X* on the top puzzle piece.

"Let's follow the wall along and look for a back entrance or something," said Lilli.

So just as she'd suggested, we followed the stony fortress wall and finally came across a pipe-like tunnel about as tall as a man which seemed to lead beneath the castle. Lilli switched on her flashlight, and we stepped inside. It smelled like mildew, and there was mud on the ground.

"I bet there are spiders and rats in here," said Marvin enthusiastically.

"Ugh, don't start that again," said Lilli.

We trudged through the mud in silence. It was pitch black apart from the beam of the flashlight. The dark, narrow tunnel made my unease grow with every step.

"Maybe even newts and frogs and bats," Marvin murmured to himself.

His carefree chatter was kind of calming. Maybe that's why Lilli let him go on. He suddenly fell silent, however, and stopped short. "Shhh," he whispered, "I hear something."

We paused and listened carefully. Voices really were coming from somewhere.

"Here," said Lilli and shone her flashlight at a little hole in the top of the tunnel. As soon as you stood directly beneath it, you could hear two men talking. They must have been members of the gang.

"Do you know who took the flag? It was here on the table before," said one of them.

"No idea. But we made copies. They're in the truck," said the other.

"Ah, who cares anyway. With our scanners we'll find the hidden room even without it," said the first.

Then the voices faded. The men above us seemed to be walking away.

"We must be under the lobby right now. That's where the flag was before," I said.

"So, a hidden room," said Lilli and shone her flashlight in our faces. "Somehow we have to get up into the castle and find that hidden room before they do. Let's go!"

Lilli ran off, deeper into the tunnel.

We followed Lilli and her flashlight whose beam was bouncing all over the place.

After only about ten feet, we really did find a way: a ladder going into a shaft leading up from the tunnel.

"Who wants to go first?" I asked.

"He who asks gets the task," said Lilli.

Narrow passages were absolutely not my thing. They made me feel like I couldn't breathe, and if I wasn't careful, I fainted. But I wanted to finally get out of this tunnel. So I took a hit from my asthma inhaler, clamped Lilli's flashlight between my teeth, grabbed the ladder and pulled myself up. The shaft felt even more narrow than it had looked from below. Spider webs caught in my hair, and rust from the ladder rungs stuck to my hands.

Soon a wooden lid blocked the way. I pressed gently on it and, to my relief, it opened upwards. I slowly stuck my head through the hole and realized immediately: We'd found our access point. I was within the walls of Bloodhound Castle.

To my amazement, it was a pit toilet that my head was sticking out of. *Marvin will get a kick out of this*, I thought to myself. Once Lilli and Marvin had climbed up, my guess was confirmed. He clapped his hands and whispered, "An old, secret escape route disguised as a toilet. How cool!"

Cautiously we opened the door. The room before us was lit softly by the moon. There was no-one here but us. Still, you could hear the muffled voices of the gang of thieves somewhere off in the distance.

Marvin tugged on my t-shirt. "Let's see that treasure map again," he whispered.

We knelt down and spread it out on the carpet.

"See that *W* on the edge of the top piece of the puzzle?" asked Marvin. "I think that symbol marks the entrance to the secret room."

"What makes you say that?" I asked.

"Look how oddly it's written. The little ticks on the beginning and end of the letter. And how unusually high the lines go on the inside of the letter."

"Get to the point," said Lilli.

"That exact symbol can be found here, in this room," he said, staring at us eyes wide.

 Where did Marvin see a *W* like the one on the treasure map?

They're Coming

The arms of the man in the big portrait over the fireplace clearly formed a *W* like on the treasure map. We figured something must be hidden behind the painting. I pulled the library ladder over, climbed up on it and tried to take the painting off the wall. But the frame wouldn't move an inch, no matter how hard I tugged. Perplexed, we stared at the picture.

"Maybe there's a secret button in the frame," said Lilli.

"Good idea," I said and used Lilli's flashlight to search it, inch by inch, for some kind of irregularity. Nothing.

Suddenly the gang's voices became menacingly loud.

"They're in the next room," whispered Marvin, pointing terrified at a closed door upholstered in red leather. "They'll be in here in a minute."

I cast one last anxious look at the portrait. Something wasn't right. But what was it? It had to do with the flashlight. It was as if it were shining through the fabric of the painting. Carefully I pressed a finger into the middle of the picture. I didn't feel any real resistance. The more I pressed, the more the canvas gave way. As if there were no wall behind it. As if…

Rip!

My finger was stuck in the middle of the masterpiece. I'd pressed too hard and torn a hole in it.

"Oops," said Lilli and grinned at me.

A few of the men in the next room laughed loudly as if agreeing with Lilli.

I didn't overthink it. I simply stuck the flashlight between my teeth so I had both hands free and tore the painting fully in half. A narrow, dead-straight shaft came into view. As did a little lever.

"There's a hidden lever here!" I yelled, grabbing it and pulling, convinced it would open a secret door.

Crack!

In my panic, I hadn't just pulled the lever. I'd yanked it right off. I stared in horror at the broken piece of wood in my hand. So much for a secret door.

"Oops," said Lilli again, this time with a reproachful undertone.

"Into the shaft then," I said, throwing the lever away and climbing in. The cavity was narrow, too narrow for an adult. That was good because it meant the gang wouldn't be able to follow us this way.

I didn't have to crawl for long. Barely were my feet into the shaft when my head was poking out the other end. At first the room before me was dim, but then lights automatically flashed on in the darkness. Within seconds everything was brightly lit, and before me lay a massive, gleaming-white hall. Monitors with all kinds of control panels were embedded around the walls, like it was some kind of spaceship. Right in the middle stood a massive half sphere which reached all the way to the ceiling and consisted entirely of mechanical robot arms. It was probably a kind of automated workbench.

"The secret room," I stammered. "An inventor's workshop."

"Unbelievable," murmured Lilli once she and Marvin had climbed in through the shaft.

We stood there in awe, taking in our surroundings.

"Hey," I whispered, "what exactly are we looking for in here?"

Without paying me any attention, Marvin yelled, "That's a mole!" He clapped his hands excitedly and ran straight for a metallic monstrosity hanging from the ceiling at the other end of the workshop. It looked like a cross between a mini-submarine and yes, a mole.

"He's off in his own world," whispered Lilli as we both stared after him in astonishment.

"Same old, same old," I murmured. "Show him an animal, and he flips out."

"You're going to flip out too in a minute," she said and pointed to a bookshelf holding a strange machine. It shimmered golden, and inside it hung a gleaming, ruby-red puzzle piece.

"That's one of the three puzzle pieces from the treasure map," I said in excitement as we stared intently at the contraption.

Four small carved skulls also hung inside, each on their own thread. The five threads each ran below a little blade which could in turn be moved by the press of a button. This enabled you to cut the thread running beneath it. A thick pane of glass prevented you from simply reaching in and grabbing anything. At the top of the contraption, the words *LOOK CLOSELY* were inscribed.

"We have to cut the right thread to make the puzzle piece fall out the hole at the bottom," said Lilli. "But what happens if we get the wrong one? If we get a skull?"

"Let's not find out," I suggested.

"It's an absolute mess. I mean, it's totally impossible," said Lilli.

Which button was the right one?

Trapped

Lilli was right. It was practically impossible to follow the paths of the threads. So the solution had to lie elsewhere: The titles of the books exactly above or beside the buttons gave us the answer. We pressed button number five, and the ruby-red puzzle piece fell right into Lilli's hand.

"The first puzzle piece is ours," she said, holding it up triumphantly.

"Then let's get out of here," I replied.

"But not back through the shaft, right? The gang might catch us," said Lilli.

Suddenly everything around us started shaking violently. Equipment, tools, monitors and the like crashed to the ground.

"What's going on?" yelled Marvin, who had already ventured inside the mole-submarine by this point.

Just then a six-foot wide, circular crack appeared in the wall beside the shaft out of which we'd just climbed.

"They're boring themselves a way in," I cried. "We've got to get out of here!"

Then the shaking stopped, and for a moment it was dead silent.

"Come over here," called Marvin. "I've found a way out."

We ran towards Marvin. Out of the corner of my eye, I saw the round piece of wall slowly falling forward. There was a deafening boom as it crashed to the ground. At practically the same time, an alarm sounded, followed by an automated announcement:

Self-destruct sequence initiated. Please evacuate. This building will self-destruct in 30...

"This can't be happening," I said.

By *25*, Lilli and I had reached Marvin.

"All aboard," he yelled, clapping his hands.

"What? What on earth for?" I cried.

Then I understood. The mole hung from the ceiling, and below it was a large hole in the ground filled with dark, stinky sludge. Swamp water. Here the mole could be lowered into the swamp and dive under like a submarine.

By *15* we were in the vehicle, and Marvin pulled the side door closed. Then he pressed a key labelled *Start* at which all the buttons and switches in the cockpit lit up green. He clutched the joystick and moved it in all directions. Every time he did, the mole jolted, but otherwise nothing happened. Then Marvin pushed a lever forwards, and the mole's paws spun ever faster. Only we weren't getting anywhere. After all, the ceiling attachment still held us suspended in midair.

There were only ten seconds left now.

"We have to get it to disconnect," yelled Lilli.

"There!" I yelled and pointed to a little screen. Over and over flashed the sentence:

Press button to release ceiling attachment.

"Hilarious," yelled Marvin, "which one? Ugh, let's just press them all!"

We hastily pushed every button we could see and opened all the protective covers to flip the toggle switches hidden beneath. They all changed colors, and the mole jerked and thrashed about, completely out of control. But none of them released the mole from the ceiling attachment.

"5," announced the loudspeaker.

"I think we've pressed them all," yelled Marvin.

"4," warned the voice.

We stared at the collection of buttons and switches before us. "3."

Then I saw it. "There's one left!" I yelled and reached for it.

Which button or switch hadn't yet been pressed?

Eyes in the Darkness

We knew from the message on the little screen that we had to find a button to release the ceiling attachment. Originally, once Marvin had activated the instruments by pressing the start button, all the buttons and switches had lit up green. After you pressed them, they changed color. Only one of the toggle switches was still glowing green. It was hidden beneath Marvin's thumb which was resting at the top of the joystick.

I unhitched the mole, and it landed with a resounding belly flop in the swamp water.

"2," said the voice.

Marvin tilted the joystick forwards and simultaneously operated the accelerator lever. The mole's nose angled downwards into the murky sludge, and its paws turned slowly.

"1," came the voice over the loudspeaker.

The paws spun visibly faster in the mud, hurling filth all across the workshop. Gradually the mole moved forwards.

"Detonation," the speaker announced casually.

The boom was deafening. We all shrieked in panic.

Through the mole's windows, I was able to watch as the entire rear portion of the workshop blew up. The half sphere of robotic arms was torn to pieces in the explosion.

The mole was now angled so steeply downwards that we started slipping forwards. At the same time, muddy swamp water rapidly engulfed the windows making it darker and darker all around us.

A second explosion followed, and not far away I could just make out the ceiling caving in before the mole became fully submerged in the swamp.

In an instant, everything was silent. All you could hear was the hum of the spinning paws, and the only illumination was from the brightly lit gauges and buttons.

"I have no idea where to go," said Marvin nervously. "But this picture on the monitor looks like the one on my flight simulator." Carefully he pulled back on the joystick and ended our descent.

"Yeah, now we're level," he said as he continued to study the instruments. "This shows whether there are any obstacles ahead of us. And this one shows what's above us. Looks like we're in a subterranean tunnel that'll lead us out to the swamp." He sounded increasingly relieved, which also calmed me and Lilli down a bit.

After travelling in silence a few minutes, Marvin decided it was time to emerge and angled the mole upwards.

When we broke through the surface, and the mud slowly slid off the glass panes, a huge weight was lifted from my shoulders. We really were in the middle of the swamp. Marvin flipped a switch, and the windows around us retracted. The fresh, balmy night air was a real relief, even if it did smell marshy. All around us insects chirped, and frogs croaked, while we took a leisurely ride by the bright moonlight and gradually pulled ourselves together.

I glanced over my shoulder and saw smoke rising from Bloodhound Castle. Then I leaned back and gazed at the stars.

As the tension faded, some questions forced their way into my mind. Why was there a self-destruct mechanism? What had activated it? Was it because of the gang's forced entry? I also wondered whether anyone had been hurt in the explosions. As I was to find out later, however, this wasn't the case.

"Look, lights! And a cottage with a jetty," said Lilli. "That'd be a good place to go ashore."

A short while later, we arrived at the dock, left the mole there and walked over to the cabin. Hopefully, whoever was inside would be kind and own a telephone.

When we reached the cottage, a shock ran right through me.

We positively froze.

A bit farther back in the shadow of a few bushes, three pairs of glowing, red eyes moved. They locked onto us.

"Don't move," whispered Lilli.

Slowly, a dog stuck its head out of the shadows and into the light, while both of the other animals remained in the background.

Marvin cocked his head, contemplating the hound. Then he examined the surroundings.

"Oh, what nonsense," he finally said in a calm voice, going to his knees and clapping his hands. "Here, doggy," he called as Lilli and I looked at each other in horror.

Why did Marvin think they were ordinary dogs and their eyes didn't really glow?

Can you figure out where the massive pawprint we saw on our way to Bloodhound Castle came from?

BONUS QUESTION

The Tall Stranger

The dog trotted over to Marvin and let him pet it. It wore some kind of goggles equipped with glowing red lights. Lilli nudged me and pointed to a workbench below the side window of the cabin. On it lay more of these glasses along with large, wooden dog paws you could slip on over your shoes.

"That's where the pawprint by the old train came from," said Lilli.

Suddenly, from the darkness behind the dogs, we heard an elderly man's voice. "Seems the youth of today aren't so easily spooked."

He stepped into the light of the cottage and we saw a friendly face peeking out from beneath a mass of white hair. Despite the warm night air, the old man had thrown a blanket around his shoulders and looked like...

"Dumbledore," whispered Lilli.

"Digby," he said. "Call me Digby."

"Hi, Digby, sir," I said hesitantly. "Why do you put those goggles on your dogs?"

The old man muttered to himself a few seconds. He seemed to be considering what to say. "Ah, what the heck," he finally replied. "It's all over now anyway."

"What's over?" I asked.

"The thing with the dogs. For several years now, I've let my dogs run through the swamp with glowing eyes. I created a legend to match the name of the old ruins, Bloodhound Castle."

"But why?" asked Lilli.

"To scare people off. The old master of Bloodhound Castle wanted to keep nosy people from the neighboring village away so he could work in peace."

"The master of Bloodhound Castle? Do you mean James Eckles? The inventor?" I asked.

"Yes," he said, eyeing us up. He seemed surprised by how much we knew. Then he went on, "But my contract wasn't extended after Bloodhound Castle was sold recently. The new owners don't want any bloodhounds."

For a brief moment we were all silent.

"You don't happen to have a phone, do you?" I asked. "We need to call our parents."

"No, I'm afraid not."

"There's a car over there," said Marvin, pointing to a rise a bit farther off. "Couldn't you drive us into the city?"

"I don't drive. The flash car with the golden hood ornament belongs to the giant in there," said Digby, nodding at the cabin. "But he can't drive right now either."

"Giant? Who is it?" I asked and slowly approached the window to peek inside.

"Brought me my last paycheck from Eckles. Must be some bigshot. His fancy red jacket probably cost more than my entire last month's wages."

"And why can't he drive right now?" I asked.

"Says he sprained his ankle. Been sitting there for hours now. Says he can't walk a single step," said Digby, clearly annoyed.

Now I could see him. Inside the cottage sat a finely dressed giant of a man searching a briefcase for something. He had his left foot resting on a stool. The red jacket Digby had mentioned lay on the arm of the chair. Something about him bothered me but for the life of me I couldn't figure out what. Lilli and Marvin peered through the window now too.

"He looks creepy," said Marvin and immediately began to draw the stranger. "We might need this."

"There is another way we can get to town," said Lilli and turned to Digby. "The street up there leads back into the city, right?"

Digby nodded. "But there's no way you can follow that street back into town. It winds through the hills, full of twists and turns. Even in a car, it's a long drive. By foot you'd be on the road all night."

Lilli gave me and Marvin a serious look and spoke so quietly now that Digby couldn't hear us. "The gang is still at the castle. They're going to leave any minute now and drive back into the city. If the truck that arrived at the castle last brings up the rear again, we might be able to jump onto the cargo bed without being noticed."

Marvin and I stared at her.

"The truck goes last because in the hills the roads are really steep, and it can only go slowly. So we'll be able to jump on back. We just need to find a steep spot," whispered Lilli and nodded as if that would convince us. She saw we still weren't sure and snorted. "We can at least try. I don't think we have any choice if we want to get home tonight."

She turned to Digby. "And if I were you, I'd watch out. If that man in there told you he couldn't walk a single step, he was lying."

 Why did Lilli think the man was quite capable of walking?

The Sphere

When we'd reached the cottage a few minutes earlier, Lilli had noticed a briefcase by the window. Now the stranger had that same briefcase on his lap and was going through it. So he must have gone to get it while we were talking with Digby.

When we got to the street, we settled in at a suitably steep spot and waited. It wasn't long before the first of the gang's cars thundered past us.

A while later the truck struggled up the road.

Lilli had been right about everything. We managed to climb onto the cargo bed in back without much difficulty. Now we sat on the floor surrounded by crates and allowed ourselves to be chauffeured back.

"As soon as we're in town and we stop at a traffic light somewhere, we'll jump out and sneak off without anyone noticing," I said.

Lilli was about to protest, when Marvin peered out over the loading ramp and said, "Can't drive my foot!"

The tall stranger's car was rapidly approaching our truck. Once he'd caught up, he slowed down and followed us. Only now did I realize the unusual, golden ornament on the hood of the car was in the shape of a lion.

"Why isn't he overtaking?" murmured Marvin.

"Because he's one of them," I said. "He's with the gang."

"If that's true and he stays on our tail, there's no way we'll be able to jump off without being seen," said Marvin.

And that's exactly what happened. The tall stranger remained hot on our heels, even once we reached town. The truck stopped twice at traffic lights, but we couldn't jump down either time, or we would have been caught on the spot. We hadn't yet given up hope that an opportunity would present itself after all, when suddenly we drove down a ramp.

"We're going into a building," whispered Marvin anxiously. "An underground car park."

Moments later the truck pulled to a stop. The voices of various gangsters echoed through the shadowy basement whose sole illumination came from a few neon lights. They must have been waiting a while and now greeted our driver boisterously.

"We can't get out," whispered Marvin. "They'll see us."

"Then let's hide. Quick, into a crate!" I said. On the truck's cargo bed stood five large, identical-looking wooden crates. I pried the lid of one of them open, and Lilli and Marvin clambered in. There was no room left for me.

No sooner had I closed the lid than I heard footsteps approaching.

Hastily I hid in the farthest corner behind a pile of spare tires.

My heart was beating like crazy. Two men opened the tailgate, jumped on and started unloading the cases and other equipment.

"While you were driving the truck over the hills at a snail's pace, we've been busy. This building is now sealed tight. No-one gets in or out. Access to all levels is electronically secured. The elevator now only goes from here up to the top floor and back. If there are civilians left anywhere in the building, they're going to have to stay put," one of them reported.

"What about the motion detectors?" asked the truck driver.

"We couldn't deactivate them. But we can sneak past. We'll go over the map of the motion detector locations again in a minute," came the answer. "And don't forget: Once we're in there, we have to find the binder labelled *Inventions: Sphere Laboratory* and take it. It's blue, yellow and red. You can't miss it. Only once we have it do we activate the self-destruct sequence here too."

Finally the men walked away from the loading ramp, but it took more than ten minutes before I stopped hearing voices and was sure I was alone.

Hesitantly I crept out of my hiding place, and it was just as I'd feared: The five crates, including the one Lilli and Marvin were in, were gone.

I climbed down from the cargo bed and looked around the dimly lit hall. The other cars were parked several feet away near a large freight elevator. The gang must have taken it up to the top floor, and their gear, including the crate with Lilli and Marvin in it, would have gone with them.

As I walked over to the large, closed elevator doors, I noticed a trestle table to their left covered in all kinds of documents. One of the pieces of paper was a schematic drawing of the building we were in. It was entitled *THE SPHERE.*

Finally I realized I knew this imposing structure in whose basement I stood. As did everyone else who lived in this region.

The Sphere was a globe-shaped building, one of the largest of its kind in the world. It contained a massive concert arena along with an exhibition center and offices. It was thirty stories high and over three hundred feet tall. The outer wall was completely made of glass.

Only a single person lived on the top story, and they went to a lot of trouble to remain anonymous. That floor was split into a living area and a staff area.

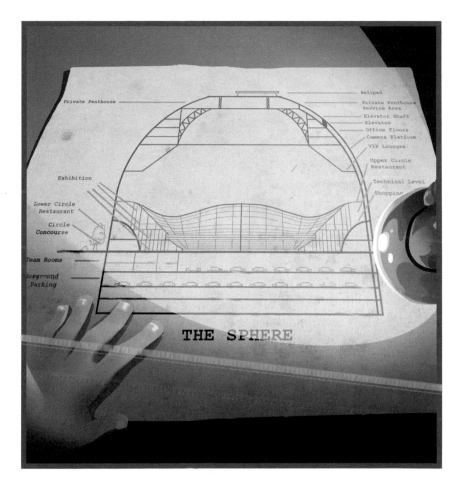

Also on the table before me lay the map the gang had mentioned showing the motion detectors in the hallways of the staff area.

Once the gang got through, I'd also have to make my way along these passages to find Lilli and Marvin in their crate. I couldn't let any of the sensors catch me or else the alarm would be set off.

I immersed myself in the map, which was color-coded to show which areas would be picked up by the motion detectors when they were in a given position. It seemed that every sensor was aimed in one direction for a few seconds and then the other.

The top part showed coverage under the first sensor alignment, the red phase, and the bottom part showed coverage under the second alignment, the green phase.

The doors seemed to all be open, so you could pass through the rooms too.

"So I go up to U17 during the red phase and then wait for the motion detectors to change direction," I said to myself. "When it gets to the green phase, I keep moving through the door on the left and on to S13." *Or should I pick another path?* After a few minutes, I was confident I'd chosen the right way through.

The elevator shot up so quickly my ears started hurting. Arriving at the top, I found myself in a reception area. Even just this first room was several times bigger than our living room at home. According to the map, the reception and the areas monitored by motion detectors were solely devoted to staff. There was a main kitchen and a secondary kitchen, various cold rooms, a rec room and accommodation facilities along with a gym for personnel, an on-call room for a medic and many other rooms. The thought that all this was just for the staff to enable them to serve a single person, the one living alone here on the top floor, was enough to make my head spin.

 Which path led me from the elevator to the private area without being caught by the motion detectors?

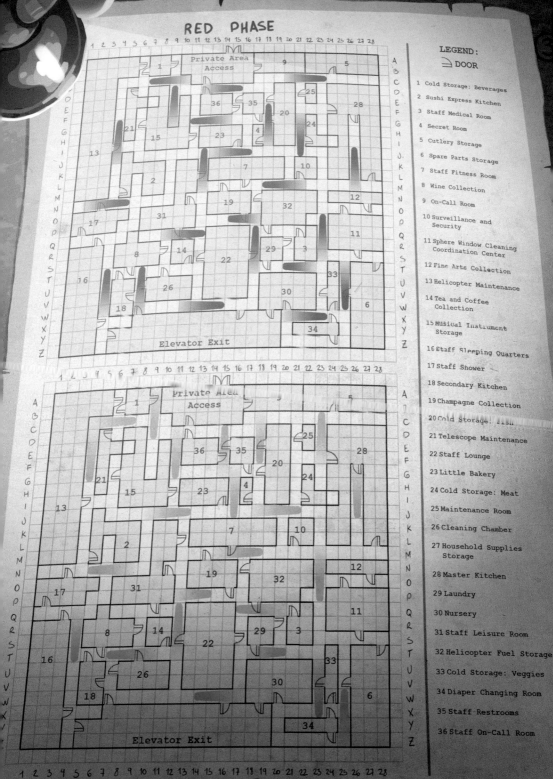

RED PHASE

GREEN PHASE

Thinking Outside the Box

I chose the following route: During the red phase, I went to W20, waited for the green phase and then made my way to V24. Then on red to T23, on green to O24, on red to M25, on green to F24, on red to D21, on green to C19, on red to G19, on green to E16, on red to E12 and finally on green all the way into the private quarters.

I stepped inside what was probably the most exclusive and expensive living space in the city. The room that now lay before me must have been the living room. Everything here was gigantic. The hanging fireplace, the observatory, the seating, the paintings, the statues, the bookcases and everything else too. But the most impressive thing was the view through the walls, which were made entirely of glass running in a high arc all the way over my head and therefore also served as a ceiling. You not only had a spectacular view of the city, but even of the starry sky above.

Suddenly I heard voices. Quick as a flash, I ducked behind a sofa and pricked up my ears. The murmuring seemed to be quite a long way off. But what now?

I fished out my walkie-talkie and spoke quietly into it. "Marvin? Lilli? Are you there?"

It took a few seconds before Lilli answered. "Timmi, where are you? We're still stuck in the crate. We can't open it from the inside. At least, not without force."

Lilli may have been whispering, but I could still hear how annoyed she was about their predicament.

"And that would make too much noise," said Marvin.

"Why are you using your own walkie-talkie? We're sitting right next to each other," grumbled Lilli.

"I like my walkie-talkie," said Marvin.

"They're exactly the same," said Lilli.

"Listen to me," I interrupted them. "We're on the top floor of the Sphere."

"Of course. I should have known," whispered Marvin. "The round outline on the treasure map. On the left puzzle piece. That's the Sphere. It's circular."

"I hadn't even thought of that," I realized in surprise. "You're right."

"Timmi, get us out of here please," said Lilli in exasperation.

"I don't know where you are and where the gang is. Somehow, I have to...," my gaze followed the glass dome all the way up, "...get an overview."

I walked on tiptoes all the way across the massive room to a glass door through which I reached a balcony. It seemed to encircle the entire Sphere. I didn't pay any attention to the view, nor to the pleasant night air. I simply concentrated on the ladder that led up the glass roof from here.

I was sure I'd be able to get a terrific overview of the rooms lying below. I'd be able to tell where Marvin and Lilli's crate was and also where the gangsters were.

I took a deep breath and another hit from my asthma inhaler, then grabbed the rungs of the ladder.

"Up we go," I told myself and began to climb.

The usual advice when you're climbing something like this is: No matter what, don't look down. But since the dome was made of glass, I guess I didn't have much choice. I was getting dizzier and dizzier. Every light breeze made me cling tightly to the ladder and pause briefly. But soon I had the view I'd hoped for. I could see the various rooms lying far below me and easily spot where each and every gangster was. They had all changed into uniforms and now looked like maintenance workers. Probably a disguise. Even though all the dark forms looked the same from up here, I thought I could make out the Hat. Clearly leader of the pack, he seemed to be giving the others directions.

That was the good news. Much to my disappointment, I also saw that the five wooden crates from the truck were in different rooms. But which one were Lilli and Marvin in?

"Hey, can you hear me?" I asked through my walkie-talkie.

"Loud and clear," said Lilli.

"Can you see anything outside your crate?" I asked. "Is there a crack or something you can see through?"

"There's a knothole here," said Lilli.

"Is the hole in one of the short sides of the crate? Or one of the long sides?" I asked.

"One of the short sides," said Lilli.

"Okay, what do you see?" I asked.

"Hmm. A bookcase, an armchair and a floor lamp," said Lilli.

"Is the lamp to the left or the right of the armchair?" I asked.

"Right," said Lilli.

"Is there a cushion on the armchair?" I asked.

"Yeah, and there's a dark-gray statue on the bookshelf."

I thought a moment. Somehow the information didn't match anything I was seeing. But then I realized which crate it must have been.

Which crate were Lilli and Marvin in?

The Right Key

Lilli could only be seeing what she described if she were in the crate in the middle room looking out the knothole at a reflection in the wall mirror.

The men were busy in other rooms, and I saw a few of them getting a massive drilling machine into position. Probably the same machine that had bored the six-foot wide hole at Blackhound Manor just before everything blew up.

"It's going to get pretty loud in a minute," I said into my walkie-talkie. "When that happens, try pushing on the lid with all your might. No-one will hear."

I'd barely finished my sentence when a terrifying racket erupted as the machine began boring into the wall. At the same time, the lid of the wooden crate began to shudder, until it finally sprang open. Lilli and Marvin climbed free.

"Okay, we're out," said Lilli. "Is the gang drilling again?"

"Yeah. They're boring themselves a way into the center of this floor. You can't see what's in there from outside," I answered. "That's probably where the second puzzle piece is hidden."

"We have to get there first," said Lilli. "What does the map say?"

"Hang on," I said, pulling the flag from my pants pocket and flattening it out on the glass dome. "I'm afraid I have no idea what position the X is supposed to mark. But on the border of the puzzle piece there's a series of numbers. A black two, a white three, a black fifty-five and a white fifty-six. Whatever that's supposed to mean."

"That could be practically anything," said Marvin.

"Oh yeah, what for example?" asked Lilli.

"Squares on a chess board," said Marvin. "They're black and white and numbered."

"Nope," replied Lilli. "They have names like A3. What else?"

"A zebra," said Marvin with a shrug.

"Timmi, you've got a good view from up there. Do you see a zebra running around anywhere?" asked Lilli. She didn't even wait for me to reply, just kept on talking. "Anything else, genius?"

"The keys on a piano," said Marvin.

Lilli went silent. When her voice came through the walkie-talkie a few moments later, it was to ask, "Timmi, do you see a piano anywhere?"

"Actually, I do," I said. "See the tall double doors? Go through."

Soon they stood beside the instrument examining its keys.

"Well, the second key is black and the third is white," said Lilli. Now she counted more keys. "The fifty-fifth is black, and the fifty-sixth is white. Incredible, Marvin."

"Play them," said Marvin, clapping his hands in excitement.

Lilli sat on the stool before the piano. We all held our breaths as she played the four notes together. The next moment, I saw a bookcase gliding aside revealing a secret passageway to the center of the floor. I cheered loudly into the night.

I quickly climbed down from the roof and snuck over to join my friends. Moments later we stepped through the secret door into the central room. Everything was vibrating in here because the gang was still trying to force their way in with their gigantic borer. We had no time to lose. After all, they could break through at any moment.

Before us lay a circular area. Just as in Bloodhound Castle, there were various computers and machines here.

"Another one of the inventor's workshops," I whispered.

But insane as it might sound, the floor beneath our feet was made entirely of glass. Far beneath us, lit up by dimmed floodlights, lay the stadium with its green grass and stands for tens of thousands of spectators. All was peaceful down there.

"Crazy," said Marvin, glancing down and walking carefully over the safety glass as if it might break at any moment.

Lilli, on the other hand, was already searching for the second piece of the puzzle. Following her example, I forced myself to concentrate. We systematically searched the room.

First, I discovered the binder the gang had mentioned labelled *Inventions: Sphere Laboratory*. It was blue with a yellow circle on the spine, in the middle of which was a red circle. I was just taking it out of a cupboard when I heard Lilli shout.

"Up there!" she yelled and pointed to a structure hanging from the ceiling like a room-sized box. It was only held up by a few supports which made it seem to float. Since the walls of this *floating room* were made of glass, you could see inside. There was a bookshelf which held the same kind of contraption we'd encountered at Bloodhound Castle. It too shone in splendid gold tones, and the second puzzle piece, which was blue, hung inside.

"Come on!" yelled Lilli and ran for the metallic scaffolding stairs that led up to the room. Marvin and I dove headlong after her and up the steps. I'd completely forgotten about the binder.

"The puzzle here is different," shouted Lilli. You could see an empty chalice and some coins. Above it was written:

How many of these coins can you put in an empty chalice like this if you put them in carefully, one after the other, and none were allowed to stick out?

Which answer was correct?

Out of the Frying Pan

In my mind's eye, I began piling up coins. At the same time, the racket from the gang's machine as they tried to bore their way in grew louder and louder. *Stay calm*, I told myself. *Concentrate.*

Suddenly there was an incredible bang, after which absolute silence descended. I looked down in fright. The gangsters had broken through, and the drilled-out piece of wall lay on the glass floor. The first of the crooks stepped through the opening in the wall and looked around.

"Onto the table!" I said. The suspended room we were in was a glass case after all, and from below they'd be able to see us walking around. Lilli and I scrambled onto the conference table, lay down flat and held our breaths.

Marvin, however, didn't seem to have even heard me. He stared at the puzzle, entranced, slowly raised a hand, stretched out his pointer finger and moved it gradually towards the contraption. Then, quite decisively, he pressed the button labelled '1', snipping the thread beside it. To my astonishment, the puzzle piece fell out of the machine and Marvin grabbed it before it hit the ground. With a huge grin, he looked over at us and said, "As soon as you've put one coin in, the chalice isn't empty anymore!" Then he noticed the panic on our faces, looked down through the glass floor and, terrified, jumped up to join us on the table.

We all lay still and waited.

More men entered the central room conversing casually. Apparently they hadn't noticed us yet.

Minutes passed.

None of them seemed interested in inspecting the seemingly empty glass box above their heads.

"I don't believe it," whispered Marvin and pointed to the cover of a magazine lying on the conference table beside us. "Look."

"That's the tall stranger who said he couldn't walk," said Lilli. She grabbed the magazine and turned to the related article.

"His name is Doctor Sangrey. It says he's the man who bought James Eckles's entire estate," she said in disbelief. "Then all this belongs to him, and Bloodhound Castle too."

"Why would he get a gang of criminals to break into his own building?" I asked.

"Okay, hang on a sec," whispered Lilli. "So the inventor James Eckles sells his entire estate, including all his inventions, to the tall stranger, this Dr. Sangrey. At the same time, he prepares everything for this treasure hunt. He disappears, but first places an ad in today's newspaper. Then the tall stranger sends criminals off to find the treasure before anyone else does."

"Does that even make sense?" I asked.

"Seems like the treasure hunt is to find the elixir Eckles developed. What if Dr. Sangrey bought the elixir off him too? What if Eckles didn't want to sell it?" said Lilli.

"You mean Eckles was forced to sell the elixir?" I asked.

"That could explain the treasure hunt. Say Eckles wants to make the elixir available to all humankind, but Dr. Sangrey is blackmailing him. So he hides it. He's hoping we, or basically anyone who isn't with Dr. Sangrey, will find it," Lilli said.

"But Dr. Sangrey sent in his gangsters," said Marvin excitedly, tearing a photo of Dr. Sangrey from the magazine and putting it in his pocket, "to either get hold of it or destroy all traces of it. That's why they blew up Bloodhound Castle."

"But they wouldn't blow up the Sphere," said Lilli. "Right?"

"Hey, that reminds me of something," I said hesitantly. "Before, when I was still hiding in the truck, I heard two of the men talking about a self-destruct mechanism up here."

"And what exactly did they say?" asked Lilli incredulously.

For the life of me, I couldn't remember. "I don't know. I was kind of overwhelmed," I whispered.

"You're messing with me," said Lilli reproachfully.

"Do you notice something?" asked Marvin.

"Timmi, you're saying you can't remember if they were planning to blow up the Sphere?" she asked again.

I shook my head.

"You're messing with me, seriously," said Lilli.

"Hey, don't you notice something?" asked Marvin, now for the second time.

"What?" asked Lilli and I in unison.

Marvin stared at us, eyes wide, and whispered, "It's too quiet."

"You're right," I murmured and peered cautiously over the edge of the table. I couldn't see a single soul below. "They're gone."

Then I realized why.

"Oh no!" I yelled and sat bolt upright.

What gave me such a fright?

CHAPTER 20

Shattered

On a monitor in the room below us, we saw the words *SELF-DESTRUCT SEQUENCE ACTIVATED*. An unmistakable warning.

Now the control unit beside us was also blinking. It was laid into the conference table we were hiding on top of. The little screen repeated the words.

Then the message changed to say that *55 seconds* remained.

"They've done it again," Lilli cursed, jumping down from the table and dashing to the door that led to the scaffolding stairs. She tugged like crazy on the door handle. "Locked!"

"I think I can unlock it from here," said Marvin and pressed a button on the control unit on the conference table.

Now, on another smaller display, you could see the words *PIN number please: - - -*. The keys below it labelled '1' through '9' lit up.

"I don't believe it," said Marvin, all the color draining from his face. "We need a three-digit code to get out of here."

"What about the ventilation duct?" said Lilli, pointing to a shaft that led from our glass room out into the external wall of the sphere.

A metal grate blocked its mouth.

Right away, she pulled a chair over and climbed onto it to reach the grate.

"You can open that from here too," said Marvin and pressed a button labeled *Maintenance Access – Ventilation Shaft*. Once more, the message requiring a PIN number flashed up. "We need the code for that too."

Lilli tugged at the grate over the shaft, but it wouldn't budge.

The larger screen now read *45 seconds*.

I stared at the number keys. There had to be some way to figure out the PIN. Marvin was about to randomly start hitting numbers when I quickly grabbed his forearm.

"Don't touch," I whispered.

I had an idea. I hastily pulled the fingerprint powder from my adventure bag. Hands trembling, I carefully applied the fine dust to the keys and then blew. It worked: A lot more powder clung to three of them than to the rest.

Marvin clapped excitedly. "Three, five and seven! Three, five and seven!"

I rapidly entered the three numbers in various orders.

The second attempt was successful: All the keys on the console lit up in green.

Without hesitation, I pressed the button to open the door.

"It's too late. We can't make it," yelled Lilli, nodding at the screen which read *12 seconds.* "Through the vent!"

She hadn't even finished her sentence when Marvin hit the corresponding button and the grate over the duct sprang open. Since Lilli was already on the chair, she immediately climbed in. Marvin was quick to follow her.

Then the countdown reached zero.

Just as I went to climb onto the chair, a series of massive explosions shook everything around me. They literally knocked me off my feet.

I lay flat on my stomach on the glass floor and watched as the circular central room below me moved away, first slowly, then faster and faster.

Initially I didn't get what was happening.

The explosions had blown the central room clean off the domed ceiling, so it, along with everything inside it, was now plummeting toward the stadium floor.

This terrifying display was accompanied by the tinkle of tons of shattering glass, the bang of breaking bricks and a deafening, metallic moan.

The glass room I was in didn't fall just yet, since it had its own mount connecting it to the ceiling.

For a moment, I thought myself safe.

But then I saw the metal steps, attached not only to the glass room but also to the crashing central room, being pulled down, twisting and screeching. Any second now they'd tear the glass box I was lying in from the ceiling and down into the abyss.

I jumped to my feet, then onto the chair and climbed into the shaft as quickly as I could, scrambling like crazy along it.

Moments later I heard a violent bang and the glass room was pulled sharply downwards, probably by the breaking staircase.

When I looked back over my shoulder, everything in there was now leaning at an angle and the conference table was sliding across the floor.

Looking ahead again, I saw Lilli lying on her back several feet ahead, stomping at another metal grate which blocked our way. It sprang from its fastenings and flew out onto the roof.

Now the shaft too was tilting noticeably, pulled downwards by the glass room as it came ever closer to falling.

Lilli made it out, followed by Marvin. I crawled hastily after them.

It was getting steeper and steeper. If you've ever climbed up a slide, you'll know what I'm talking about.

Just as I reached the opening that led onto the roof and started pulling myself out, the shaft tore off and fell into the depths. My torso was already on the dome, but my legs still dangled in the air. Lilli and Marvin pulled me to safety.

We quickly looked back through the hole into the Sphere. Below us was a three-hundred-foot void at the bottom of which lay a scene of utter devastation. The glass room we'd been inside until just moments ago was in free fall.

Then it smashed upon the field in the stadium and became part of the wreckage.

❖ ❖ ❖

Eventually we crawled farther up the dome and found ourselves on a helipad. We were completely exhausted and didn't say a thing to one another at first. For a while, we just lay there.

Soon sirens approached. The police. The fire brigade. Ambulances too, although thankfully, as we were to find out later, no-one was hurt.

The heavens gradually turned lilac and the stars faded. We sat up and enjoyed the first rays of sunlight on our faces.

The streets all around were blockaded. Curious onlookers gathered behind the barriers and stared at the badly damaged Sphere. Lilli grabbed her binoculars and turned the tables on them by peering back.

"Look at all those people," she said. Then she seemed to spot something. "You're not going to believe this."

"After everything that's happened today? Nothing could surprise me at this point. What is it?" I asked wearily.

"That Doctor Sangrey," she replied. "I think he's still down there. He's waiting nearby to see how it all turns out, just like he did at Bloodhound Castle."

 Why did Lilli think Dr. Sangrey was down there?

Grounded

Although you couldn't see the car very clearly, it was highly likely it belonged to Dr. Sangrey, because it had a golden hood ornament. Once Lilli had increased the magnification on her binoculars, she could also make out two bits of red cloth jammed in the front door. The fabric gleamed in the same eye-catching color as the jacket Dr. Sangrey had thrown over the arm of his chair in the cottage near Bloodhound Castle.

A short while later, a rescue helicopter landed on the Sphere's helipad and picked us up. It was the first time we'd ever flown in one. Marvin was suddenly wide awake again. They let him sit next to the pilot, and he spent the entire flight irritating him with random bits of half-knowledge he'd picked up from computer games.

Eventually our parents were notified. They had already reported us missing and were extremely relieved to have us back.

The police wanted to know exactly what had happened. We told them everything, not failing to mention the tall stranger we'd identified as Dr. Sangrey. Marvin showed Inspector Hallewell the drawing he'd done of Dr. Sangrey in the cottage near Bloodhound

Castle along with the photo from the article we'd found in the Sphere.

The inspector looked like she was kicking herself. Perhaps because she hadn't made the squad car wait longer at Bloodhound Castle. Perhaps because she hadn't foreseen us going off on our own to investigate. Perhaps because she hadn't taken us seriously enough.

Not willing to make the same mistake twice, she promised to pay Dr. Sangrey a visit today to question him, even though it was Sunday. She soon found out where Dr. Sangrey was at that moment. He'd proclaimed inventor James Eckles's former country estate to be his personal headquarters. Inspector Hallewell decided to pay him a visit around five that evening.

Of course, there was no way we wanted to miss out on that conversation, and we insisted on tagging along. After everything we'd been through, we deserved some answers, we told her. Our parents said it was out of the question though. They declared our adventure officially over.

But before we went home, we coaxed a promise out of Inspector Hallewell: If we could manage to get our parents' permission to be there for Dr. Sangrey's interrogation, then she'd let us listen in on it.

Back at home, I was finally able to get some sleep. By around three in the afternoon, I lay awake in bed and stared at the ceiling. In two hours, Inspector Hallewell would arrive at Dr Sangrey's country estate. Of course, my parents wouldn't even think about letting me out of the house.

But we were so close. We had two of the puzzle pieces from the treasure map. Lilli had told us over and over not to let the police know about them yet, so she still had one of the pieces and Marvin the other. If only we knew where the third was hidden.

Suddenly, I heard my walkie-talkie crackle.

"Timmi, are you awake?" asked Marvin.

I leapt straight out of bed, grabbed it and answered, "Yep, I'm here."

"We're outside your house with our bikes. Can you come out?" asked Lilli.

That meant I'd have to sneak out. But I had no choice. If we wanted to find the treasure before time ran out, we had to go now.

"Okay, give me a couple of minutes," I said and quickly grabbed my things. This time I wrote my parents a note too, telling them we were on our way to join Inspector Hallewell for the interrogation. Which was actually the truth. I placed the note in my bed.

Then I opened my window and was about to climb out, when suddenly I grew wary. Taking the garden path wouldn't be such a good idea after all. It seemed my father was expecting that.

What made me wary?

The Lion's Den

A shadow, no doubt my father's, had caught my eye. He'd probably settled in with a book behind the tree so he could catch me if I tried to sneak out. But he was out of luck. Because now that I knew where he was, I simply slipped out the front door. There I grabbed my mother's bike and off I went. Lilli, Marvin and I were united once more.

The journey to Dr. Sangrey's country estate went through fields and meadows, past ripe corn and fruit trees, and over little wooden bridges and the streams flowing beneath them. We felt happy, free and alive.

Inspector Hallewell looked quite surprised when she saw us waiting by the large cast-iron gate barring the mansion's driveway. But she kept her word. She let us hop into her squad car and together we drove up the pebble-covered path to the lion's den.

The building looked enormous. The front was reminiscent of a grand castle that could once have belonged to a king. It was totally different from creepy, dingy old Bloodhound Castle. Parklike grounds extended to either side of the mansion.

Uniformed servants opened the squad car doors and one of them accompanied us inside. The air there was cool, and it smelled freshly cleaned. The furnishings were almost entirely made of dark wood, shimmering like silk. Here and there stood statues and sculptures. Massive paintings hung on the high walls along with gigantic rugs I'd have expected to see on the gleaming marble floor instead. This was a whole new world to us.

The servant strode ahead and led us through a multitude of rooms, all the way up to a large wooden door on which he now knocked. A light on the wall next to it turned green.

"The master is expecting you," he said as the door magically swung open.

Inspector Hallewell walked in ahead of us. We entered a kind of office. The middle of the room was occupied by an ominous-looking writing desk, behind which sat 'the giant', Dr. Sangrey. He had one leg elevated, probably because of the injury he'd sustained at the cottage by the swamp. He wore comfy-looking slippers and beside him there was a pair of crutches.

"Are they yours?" he asked the inspector, meaning us.

She shook her head. "No. These kids say they saw you last night at Bloodhound Castle and this morning in the vicinity of the Sphere, I thought I'd bring them along." Then she turned to us. "Well, kids, is this really the man you say you saw?"

Instead of answering, I decided to turn the tables, asking, "Were you at Bloodhound Castle yesterday and in the vicinity of the Sphere this morning?"

Although I couldn't make out Dr. Sangrey's eyes because his face lay half in shadow, I could still feel his piercing glare.

"Last night at Bloodhound Castle? Yes. This morning in the vicinity of the Sphere? No," Dr. Sangrey finally said with a decisive nod.

"You bet he was there," whispered Marvin.

Suddenly, I realized why I'd had such a bad feeling when I'd seen Dr. Sangrey in the cottage near Bloodhound Castle that first time. The same uneasy feeling crept over me again now. It was his eyes. And his mouth. You couldn't make them out. They were black, as if they were constantly in the shadows. Just like in the legend of the Guardians of the Dark Power. A chill ran down my spine. Dr. Sangrey wasn't one of the Guardians, was he?

"Could you..." My voice faltered. I took a deep breath. "Could you please step into the light a bit more? So we can see your face better?"

My pulse raced. Again I felt his piercing glare. But now I gathered up all my courage and stared defiantly back.

He didn't move. Instead he said, "You're the kids who found that pirate's treasure a while back. The inventor James Eckles, in whose former home we're now standing, acquired many of the items from your discovery. Did you know that? He dedicated himself to studying them day and night, like a man obsessed. And now he has suddenly gone missing." He paused and then went on, "Some things are better left undisturbed, I guess."

For a few seconds, a sinister silence reigned. Had he just threatened us?

Only now did I notice the newspaper beside him. It was open to the page with the ad for the treasure hunt.

"But the Guardians plan to hide it away," I quoted the riddle from the newspaper, my voice trembling. "You're one of them, aren't you? The Guardians of the Dark Power."

"Guardians of the Dark Power," Dr. Sangrey repeated almost pensively. Then he gave a cold smile and said, "Close the door behind you, hmm?"

How rude, I thought to myself. *Kicking us out just like that.*

"This morning, I still wasn't sure it was you outside the Sphere. But now I'm certain!" said Lilli. "It wasn't just your hands you got dirty."

What did Lilli notice? What did she mean by "It wasn't just your hands you got dirty."?

The Guardians

Lilli explained how she'd seen a car outside the Sphere that morning with red fabric sticking out the bottom of the front door. The jacket hanging in the office, which belonged to Dr. Sangrey and was the same red color, had clearly visible smudges of dirt in exactly the right spots: between the third and fourth holes in the belt and on the corner of the jacket. That couldn't be a coincidence. Still, Inspector Hallewell sent us out of the room now, deeming this to be anything but reliable evidence and preferring to continue her interrogation alone.

No sooner had the heavy, wooden office door closed behind us than we all began to talk at once.

"He's one of the Guardians!" I said. "Did you see his eyes?"

"You couldn't even see them!" said Marvin.

"James Eckles was studying our treasure!" said Lilli. "Now we know for sure. James Eckles somehow got hold of the book we found back then and made the elixir described in it a reality."

"Now it all makes sense. On our last adventure, the Guardians wanted to stop us finding the book about the elixir. Then when we did, they stole it straight back off us. Now they want to stop the elixir itself from coming to light," I concluded.

"But James Eckles wants the world to have it," said Lilli.

"So the Guardians somehow made him sell all his property to Dr. Sangrey so they could keep the elixir for themselves," I added.

"And they forced him to disappear forever," whispered Marvin.

"But he didn't give them the satisfaction," I said. "He hid the elixir somewhere first and made sure it could be found using the newspaper ad and the treasure map."

"And when Dr. Sangrey found out, he sent the gang to snap up the treasure map and destroy all the places shown on it," said Lilli.

"So no-one would ever be able to find the elixir," said Marvin.

I got a horrible feeling we'd messed up. "We just blew our cover," I said. "Up till now Dr. Sangrey didn't know anyone else was after the treasure."

"How could we be so stupid," said Marvin, slapping himself on the forehead.

"Okay, now we have to find the third piece of the puzzle, quick," said Lilli. "Remember the rhyme from the newspaper ad? *The elixir breaks down tomorrow, 10 p.m. Unless you manage to save it by then.* We've only got about four hours left. And we have no idea where it is."

Lilli was right. Things weren't looking good.

"But this might help," she said, holding up a folded piece of paper. "It's a map of the city center. I brought it with me from home. Look: The treasure map shows the outline of the building we're looking for. It's shaped like an M. If it's a big building, we might be able to see it on this map."

We decided to look at the map out in the fresh air. Arriving outside, we sat down on the gravel in front of the big entrance steps. The afternoon sun shone on our faces and the scent of freshly mown grass hung in the balmy breeze blowing over to us from the massive gardens.

None of us were in the mood to enjoy the weather though. We had spread both the treasure map and the city map out before us, weighted the corners down with stones and were staring at it.

Only it didn't help. We couldn't find any M-shaped buildings.

"Maybe it's not in the city center. It could be in the countryside," I said, discouraged.

"Yeah. In that case we could search this map forever," replied Lilli. "It only shows the city center."

"Don't give up," I said. "We have to concentrate. Find the M."

"Look, there are bunnies over there," Marvin suddenly yelled, clapping his hands excitedly.

"Now? Really?" I asked.

Marvin saw that Lilli and I couldn't share his enthusiasm right then. "I need a break," he said, jumping up, grabbing his sketch pad and running over to the hill where some rabbits were hopping around. Sadly, they hid when they saw Marvin coming. He stopped where he was, his face falling, and watched them lollop away. Then he kept walking up the hill till he came to a place with a terrific view. There he finally sat down under a tree and sketched Dr. Sangrey's country estate.

"*Close the door behind you,*" I said, repeating Dr. Sangrey's words. "Very funny."

"That was really creepy just now," Lilli said. "You know, his eyes and mouth."

"Maybe it was just the way he was standing. In the shadows," I said and tossed a pebble.

"Why would there be people with pitch-black eyes and mouths?" she asked. "Why do the Guardians so desperately want to keep the elixir a secret?

Lost in thought, we continued to stare at the maps as they fluttered gently in the wind.

"Guess what?" asked Marvin, suddenly appearing behind us and giving us an awful fright. "I've got it! Now I know where to look."

Why did Marvin think he had found the M-shaped building?

Just a Little Look Around

From the top of the hill, Marvin had noticed the large M above the front door. Then he realized that the shape of the building he'd drawn was also like an M. On his way back to join us, he then also spotted an M on the servants' uniforms. We later found out the name of the estate. It was *Castle M*.

"According to the map, the room we're looking for should be in the left-hand corner at the back of the castle," said Lilli. "That's where we'll find the golden puzzle piece. Then we'll have all three."

We went back inside and strolled as discreetly as we could from room to room. After passing through many almost identical-looking, magnificently furnished rooms, Marvin suddenly stopped short in front of a plain, white door with a window in it. A sign said: *Flying Inventions Hangar*. Curious, he peeked through the window.

"Well slap me with bread and call me a sandwich," whispered Marvin, flinging the door open and stepping through.

I too was awestruck. Before us lay a gigantic hall. The ceiling was as high as a ten-story building, and it was so vast in width and length that people walking at the other end looked as small as ants. The opposite end of the hall was open to the outdoors. Beyond it stretched the parklike grounds surrounding the estate.

Right by where we stood were various bizarre flying machines. They seemed to be inspired by animals. One aircraft resembled a dragonfly, another a bat, the next a mosquito, the one next to that a butterfly, and there were many more.

Marvin ran straight over to a big, fat bumblebee, an almost perfectly spherical machine whose ability to fly I strongly doubted. Through the bumblebee's eyes you could see the cockpit.

Marvin clambered in. Hopefully he wouldn't touch anything.

"Timmi, look at this," said Lilli, fascinated. "I wish I could build stuff like this."

I hardly heard Lilli; I was much too busy worrying about Marvin.

"Come on, look," said Lilli and gave me a little kick on the foot. She was holding a small robotic bird in her hand which really looked incredibly lifelike.

"Lilli, put that back. Everything here must be worth a fortune," I said. I had to keep raising my voice, because a muffled rumbling noise suddenly emanated from my right.

Please don't let that be Marvin, I thought and glanced back at him. I saw him sitting in the cockpit of the bumblebee, beaming with enthusiasm as its mechanical wings caused the noise and also some wind. Marvin had switched on the engine.

"Uh-oh," said Lilli.

Some of the flying machines parked around the bumblebee began to wobble precariously, knocked about by the wind its wings were causing. Lilli and I gestured like crazy at Marvin to turn it off. He waved gleefully and increased the wing speed. The bumblebee slowly lifted off.

"Uh-oh," repeated Lilli.

Then the bumblebee began to spin on its own axis, coming dangerously close to other flying machines in the process. Marvin managed to stop the rotation, but then he pulled to the left. The wind created by the movement blew two flying machines over at once, sending them crashing to the ground. Marvin pulled back to the right, which only served to knock several flying machines into each other on this side too. The hall was filled with the sound of crashing and shattering.

Stunned, I stared at the bumblebee and the surrounding scene of destruction. Marvin now seemed to notice the chaos he'd caused. At least his face looked panicked as he carefully brought the bumblebee down again and switched off the engine.

"You were saying I should put this back carefully, right?" asked Lilli, holding up the little robotic bird. "So nothing valuable here gets broken, hmm?"

Marvin ran over to us. "Sorry," he yelled. "I need more practice."

"Practice?" I asked, aghast. "Practice?"

"Come on, we've got to get out of here," said Lilli, tugging on my sleeve.

People were now running at us from all over the vast hall. Most of them wore overalls. You could tell by their cries they were in quite a flurry.

Almost exactly at that moment, an alarm rang out overlaid every few seconds by an announcement: "Warning. Please leave the building. This is not a drill."

We hightailed it out the door we'd come in through and raced towards the room the last puzzle piece was meant to be in according to the treasure map. It was, as we discovered after our almost two-minute sprint, easy to find this time: The door sported the same spiral pattern as decorated the edge of the third puzzle piece on the treasure map. It was some kind of archive for antique artefacts. And right in the middle, the contraption with the golden puzzle piece awaited us along with the next riddle. It went:

I'm not alive, but I can grow. I have no lungs, but I need air. I have no hands, but I hate touching water.

"It's a what-am-I riddle," whispered Lilli. "One of the pictures on the buttons must be the answer. An apple, a balloon, a cloud, a ship or a fire. I think I know which one. What do you think?"

Which of the pictures was the answer to the riddle?

Heavily Guarded

The answer to the riddle was fire. It can spread and grow, but to do that it needs air. You can put it out with water. Lilli pressed the button and the third puzzle piece fell into her hand.

"We've got them all," I whispered and saw the excitement on my friends' faces.

"But what now?" asked Lilli.

"Let's put them together," Marvin suggested enthusiastically.

We lay the three pieces of the puzzle on the ground. My hands were shaking. Nervously, I joined the first two pieces. When I added the third and final piece and gently pressed, they snapped into place with an audible *click*. The three puzzle pieces became a single, round disc.

Just then the disc started speaking. "Hello? Hello, who's there?"

We all got a huge fright and backed away from it.

"What is *that*?" asked Marvin.

"Some kind of walkie-talkie," Lilli guessed, leaning over the disc. "Who are you?"

"James Eckles. I'm James Eckles. Don't say you're kids?"

"We finished your treasure hunt and found all the puzzle pieces," said Lilli.

"That's... that's... unbelievable," stuttered Eckles. "I wasn't expecting kids."

"Where are you?" I asked. "Where's the elixir?"

"The elixir," mused Eckles. "Yes, well, it's hidden in the Museum of Technology. In one of the exhibit pieces from my collection."

"No way," said Marvin. "We were there right at the beginning!"

"Which one is it?" asked Lilli.

"The piece is called *Countdown.* There's a big digital sign showing the number of seconds left. You can't miss it."

"I know that one," I said. "I noticed it when we were there."

"Well, the elixir is inside it, cooled to below negative two hundred degrees Fahrenheit. This cooling requires power, and when at ten o'clock tonight the time is up, the power will have been fully depleted. Then the elixir will deteriorate into a simple thirst quencher."

"We've got just over three hours," whispered Marvin.

"Yes, but I'm afraid it's not as simple as that," Eckles went on. "Only I can stop the countdown. And I can't make it there. Unfortunately, I've been abducted."

"Who abducted you? The Guardians?" I asked.

"Yes, the Guardians of the Dark Power. You're incredibly well informed," said Eckles. "They dragged me away to one of their ancient lairs. Even if you could set me free, you'd never make it in time."

"And where is this lair?" asked Lilli.

"Around sixty miles north of my old country estate."

"Sixty miles?" I said. "It'd take us the whole day on our bikes."

"Even if someone drives us, we won't make it," said Lilli.

"I know how we can get there," Marvin said, clapping his hands.

We stared at him in amazement. *How?* Then I realized what he was thinking.

"Absolutely not!" I protested and looked at Lilli. She just shrugged.

❖ ❖ ❖

A short while later, I found myself in a rumbling bumblebee. Fields and meadows rushed by beneath us as we flew about fifteen feet off the ground, piloted by a euphoric Marvin. I was pretty uneasy because we were going insanely fast.

"I can't condone this, kids," said Eckles through the puzzle walkie-talkie.

"The steering is really intuitive," said Marvin. "Everything's under control."

"That's true. I was pretty happy with how it turned out," said Eckles, sounding quite proud.

A few minutes earlier, we'd hastily sneaked back to the bumblebee. The alarm announcement had ordered the employees to leave the estate, so we hadn't run into a single soul. Eckles told Marvin the coordinates of the dungeon where he was being held captive and helped him enter them into the bumblebee's system. Our destination now appeared on a small, computer-generated map and Marvin headed straight for it.

"You should land soon and go the rest of the way by foot so the guards don't see you," Eckles warned us. "Actually, you really should notify the police and wait for them."

"You must have said that at least ten times in the past quarter of an hour," said Lilli. "We can't. We wouldn't make it back to the elixir in time."

"Out of the question," said Marvin.

Soon afterwards, he set the bumblebee down in a meadow. We made a cross-country dash till we came to a hill. From here you had a good view of the land in front of the ancient dungeon.

"I only see one guard," I whispered.

"No. No, there are more than that," said Lilli. "I think there are four in total."

Why did Lilli think there were four guards down below?

The Dungeon

Lilli was right, of course. One guard sat in plain sight. Opposite him sat the second, holding his campfire bread close to the flame. The third was busy in one of the porta potties. Lilli made this assumption based on the red 'occupied' sign on the door. A fourth guard's outline could be seen under the tree by the entrance to the dungeon.

"I'm somewhere in there," said Eckles over the puzzle walkie-talkie.

"It looks like an archeological dig site," I said.

"Yes, it really is an ancient dig site with underground tunnels," said Eckles. "The main entrance is up top. That's where we came in. My dungeon is inside the facility. You can access the area through a metallic door. If the door is locked, you'll have to find another way of getting in. I do think I saw some old ventilation ducts you could get in through, but then you might end up in an ancient part of the facility that hasn't been set foot in for centuries. That would be simply irresponsible."

"He's right," I said. "It would be too dangerous."

"Only if they catch us, Timmi," said Lilli and ran off without a second's hesitation.

Marvin stared after her. "It's always the same with Lilli."

"Always the same," I agreed and followed her.

We made it to the main entrance undetected and stepped inside a cavernous lobby. Pieces of equipment lay all around, probably stuff that was necessary when exploring such old structures. So there were, for example, glowsticks, which are plastic tubes around ten inches long that light up brightly for a while after you snap them. Nearby we also saw modern lamps, ropes and climbing gear, chalk for marking stored items, and much more. We grabbed ourselves some flashlights and glowsticks.

At the back was the heavy, metal door Eckles had mentioned. It was sealed tight. There didn't seem to be any way of opening it. Eckles confirmed that it led to the corridor along which his dungeon lay.

"Look to your left, in the shadow of the rock face," he said. "I thought I saw something that looked like an air duct there."

Sure enough there was a dark, old shaft that led downwards about as steeply as a slide. Inside it was angular rather than round and not much wider than my shoulders. We'd just fit.

"Oh, great," I said as I shone a flashlight down into the darkness. Its light didn't reach the end.

"Give me a glowstick," I told Marvin, who handed me one. I snapped it across my knee, at which a soft, blue light spread through the little tube. Then I tossed it down the shaft. At first it jumped around like crazy on its way down, but in the end it just rolled. And rolled and rolled. Then it fell out of sight.

"That must be more than sixty feet," I whispered.

"Let's use the rope," said Lilli. She tied a long, thick climbing rope to a heavy machine with a sailor's knot.

"Hang on. Before we go down there, I want to know what the elixir actually does," I told Eckles. "Why is it so important?"

"It's a healing potion," whispered Lilli, as if that were what she wanted to hear.

There was a long pause. Eckles hesitated. "It is a healing potion, yes," he said finally. "For hay fever."

"For *hay fever*?" cried Lilli incredulously. "Nonsense. You just don't want us to put ourselves in danger."

"No, that's all it is. Hay fever is a horrible affliction," said Eckles.

"We're getting you out now," said Lilli. "Then you owe us the truth."

Lilli and Marvin lowered me down on the rope. I slid slowly deeper and deeper into the pitch-black shaft.

The air was stuffy, and I grazed my back more and more with every foot that passed. The puzzle walkie-talkie was attached to my chest. I took a hit from my asthma inhaler and decided to take my mind off my discomfort.

"Why didn't you just call the police yourself?" I asked Eckles. "After all, you have a two-way radio you're using to talk to us."

"Because it only works on this specific frequency. Unless someone else just happens to use that frequency, which practically never happens, only we can communicate over it."

"Got it. Next question," I went on. "If we don't make it to the elixir in time, can't you just make another batch?"

"To do that I'd need a specific, ancient book which is in the hands of the Guardians. Without the book and my records, I could only make another batch of the elixir using the sample I hid at the museum. If we don't get to it in time, it's all over. Then the Guardians will be the only ones who'll be able to produce it, thanks to my research."

I was about to ask him about the ancient book he'd mentioned when I felt my feet reach the end of the shaft.

Carefully I slid to the floor of the room.

It was eerily still down here and completely dark except for the light from the glowstick and my flashlight. My feet left footprints in the dust. No-one else had been down here in a long time.

Two sides of the room had tall stone doors but only one of the two was ornately decorated.

Fascinated, I stared at the picture carved into the stone. I thought it looked like a pirate's head. At the top of the door, I could make out an inscription. I read it out quietly:

Only those who can turn their perspectives upside-down may pass.

"That sounds like an illusionist test," said Eckles. "Suits this place. It was probably originally built by followers of the illusionist cult before the Guardians of the Dark Power took it over for their own purposes. If that's the case, then you're going to have to pass a total of three of these tests to get to the other end of the facility."

"Three tests," I murmured.

"We have to hurry," said Lilli once she and Marvin had caught up with me. "Before we got into the shaft, we heard a helicopter. I think Dr. Sangrey sent his gang after us. He must have realized we took off in the bumblebee and put two and two together."

"It won't be long before they notice the rope we tied up there and see it leads into the ventilation shaft," said Marvin.

"They won't fit through the shaft," I pointed out.

"But there might be another way down we don't know about," said Lilli.

"As if we weren't in enough of a rush already," I said. "Okay, see the animals on the stone buttons by the door? The answer must be an animal."

Lilli and I exchanged a meaningful look and shone our flashlights in Marvin's face.

"Your specialty," Lilli said with a smile.

"It's an optical illusion." He gave us a mischievous grin and confidently pressed one of the buttons. "Don't you see it?"

 Which button did Marvin press?

Appearances Are Deceiving

Marvin was dead right. It was an optical illusion. First you saw a terrifying face. But if you turned it up the other way, it became a cat in a basket. Once Marvin pressed the cat button, the door rumbled as it was drawn up by an automatic mechanism. Beyond it lay a long, dark passageway.

"Guess we don't have much choice," I said and shone my flashlight into the darkness.

All of a sudden, we heard a loud noise behind us. To our horror, we saw the door on the other side of the room opening with a groan.

"Oh no!" whispered Lilli. "The gang."

"Go, go, go!" I yelled and we ran into the passageway before us.

After a few steps, we heard a quiet click.

"Pressure plate," said Marvin. "We stepped on a pressure plate."

Bang!

The heavy stone door we'd just passed through crashed to the floor. Dust and stone chips flew through the tunnel.

"Oops," said Lilli.

"At least now the gang has to solve the riddle before they can chase us," I said. "We'll see how well they manage."

"You better hurry," came Eckles's voice from the puzzle walkie-talkie. "But watch where you step. There might be more traps."

We shone our flashlights on the ground.

"Oh boy," I said.

Then we walked on, quickly but carefully.

"So what's the story with this elixir anyway?" Lilli asked Eckles. "Now that we're down here, you might as well tell us the truth."

Eckles sighed. "Well, the effects are highly complex. We hardly had the time or the opportunity to really investigate it properly. But in a nutshell, it opens the mind," he said.

"It *what*?" asked Lilli.

"Imagine you flicked through your math textbook just once and immediately not only understood everything but also committed it permanently to memory. You could learn whatever you liked in a very short time. Playing the piano or some kind of sport, for example. You'd be done in a matter of hours. A full medical degree in a matter of days. The possibilities are endless."

"I want that," said Marvin. "I want to be the best artist in the world. And the best vet!"

"Well, if everyone had access to this elixir, soon everyone would be extremely good artists if they wanted to be," said Eckles.

"So even then I wouldn't be anything special," whispered Marvin mournfully.

"You wouldn't be any more or less special than you are already, little man," said Eckles. "But an elixir that was freely accessible to everyone would significantly change humanity. Including our coexistence, not only in our little neighborhoods but the world over too. The elixir carries great opportunities but also equally great risks."

"What exactly do you mean?" I asked.

"Who knows where a development like this might lead? Wouldn't it be unnatural? And what if not everyone had equal access to the elixir? Wouldn't that be yet another factor leading to terrible inequality?"

"You sound like you're not so sure yourself," I said.

"Oh yes, absolutely," said Eckles. "Only if it's not reserved for the lucky few but is made available to the whole of humanity, then the elixir is something positive."

Somehow I wasn't quite so sure of that.

"Of course, it's debatable," Eckles admitted. "But one thing is for sure: If the Guardians of the Dark Power are the only ones who can use the elixir, they'll build up limitless power on the backs of others."

Lilli, Marvin and I stared at one another. That made sense.

After a few minutes, the passage opened into another room at the end of which stood a door with a picture and inscription. It read:

Only those who can take some distance when looking at life's challenges may pass.

"The second test," I said. "Eckles said there'd probably be three altogether."

On the floor in front of the door lay stone plates with cryptic, unfamiliar characters.

"If that's another optical illusion, I can't figure it out," said Marvin, cocking his head to one side.

 Which was the correct floor plate to choose?

The Last Test

I was absolutely fascinated by the sight before me. How could the picture change just because you stood farther away from it? It was simply unbelievable. Marvin, however, didn't see the difference.

"It's probably the artist in you," I said. "It's not so easily fooled."

Lilli stepped onto the stone plate at the top right from where we were standing. The door opened with a rumble. Once more, a dark tunnel stretched out before us.

At that moment we heard the soft echo of footsteps. Someone was running. In the darkness of the passageway through which we'd entered the room just before, wildly waving lights approached.

"They're coming," whispered Lilli.

"Where's the pressure plate?" I asked. "To close the door."

We dashed into the tunnel and searched. Marvin found it and stepped onto it. But the door didn't move.

Suddenly the first man shot out of the passageway opposite and ran like a maniac across the room towards us. It was their leader, the Hat. In a few moments, he'd reach us.

"Get on the pressure plate!" yelled Marvin, waving us over.

Lilli and I ran over to him and all three of us stomped on the stone floor trigger together. Still nothing happened.

We saw with horror that the man would soon be at the door.

"Get off!" I yelled. "We have to get off for it to work!"

We leapt off the plate and finally heard the familiar *click*.

The door slammed to the ground just inches before the fast-approaching gang leader. We heard him cursing through the door.

"That was close," I said, my heart pounding in my chest.

"Come on, let's go. This time I bet they'll solve the puzzle faster," said Lilli.

We shone our flashlights down the dark passageway before us.

"Let's just run all the way this time," I suggested.

At that moment, the loud rumble of the door opening again rang out behind us. They'd solved the puzzle just like that!

"No way," yelled Lilli, sounding more angry than scared. "You're staying out!" She stamped once hard on the pressure plate. There was a *click* and the door crashed back down again.

"That's how we'll slow them down," said Lilli. "You two run on to the third test. Call me when you've solved the puzzle."

Seeing the looks on our faces, she seemed to realize Marvin and I weren't happy to leave her behind.

"Go!" she yelled, furious, as the door rose again with a rumble.

"Be careful," I said.

Then we ran for our lives. After about half a minute we reached the third room. As expected, another engraved door stood at the end of it.

❖ ❖ ❖

Meanwhile, Lilli had already activated the pressure plate three times, causing the stone door to fall back down. Each time she waited for the gap to be open about ten inches. Too small for a fully-grown adult to squeeze through. It was almost time again now.

Suddenly a bright light shone through the opening into the passage, blinding her. The gang was trying to figure out what was going on on the other side. She promptly stomped on the pressure plate and the stone door cut off the light as it thundered to the ground.

Lilli stared at it. She was sure the men would press the button again soon, making it rise once more. But nothing happened. That was suspicious. It was taking much longer than the last four times. Had they given up? The silence was unnerving. But whatever the case, Lilli was going to wait.

❖ ❖ ❖

At about the same time, Marvin and I were staring at the inscription for the third test. It read:

Only those who can see things from unusual points of view may pass.

We cocked our heads and varied our distances from the picture but couldn't figure out the solution.

❖ ❖ ❖

Soon afterwards, the door before Lilli rumbled into motion once more. Same old thing after all. The gap was now open four inches. This time, no bright light shone into the passageway. Eight inches. In a moment Lilli would stamp on the pressure plate.

Then something moved in the gap. Lilli hesitated at first, then quickly stomped on the trigger, but it was too late. To her horror, the door only descended a little then stopped, stuck. The men had shoved something in the gap to hold it open. The first gangster immediately tried squeezing through and Lilli could see he was going to make it.

❖ ❖ ❖

Just at that moment, Marvin yelled, "I've got it," and stomped on one of the pressure plates.

Which word did Marvin see in the etching?

CHAPTER 29

The Prisoner

Marvin had looked at the picture from the right at a very sharp angle. (It worked from below too.) From that perspective, the apparently random lines suddenly formed the word PUMUCKLIMUNSO. Now there he stood on the matching pressure plate.

"Hurry, they're coming," we suddenly heard Lilli shout as she sprinted in from the passageway. "They're right behind me!"

The door wasn't even two feet open yet, but we immediately crawled through the gap.

There a surprise awaited us.

Instead of a further dark passageway, we found ourselves in a circular room with a lofty ceiling. In the center stood a podium upon which a sculpture of an eagle gleamed. It was studded with all kinds of jewels.

"What's going on?" we heard Eckles ask. "What do you see?"

"An eagle covered in gems, about as big as a football," I said, searching for the pressure plate that had lain behind each door so far to shut them. But this time there was nothing.

Instead I heard the footsteps of a man running like crazy. They quickly got closer.

"An elevator," yelled Lilli. "Get in!"

She pointed to a wooden cage off to the side of the room. Ropes led from the top of it all the way up to the high ceiling. There you could see a kind of platform. It had to be our way out. We all ran for the antique contraption.

"You're now in the treasure chamber," Eckles went on untroubled. "That's where whatever this facility is meant to protect is stored. Don't touch anything, whatever you do. If you try to take the eagle, it's sure to trigger a booby trap."

"That's the least of our worries right now," yelled Lilli as we sprinted into the cage.

We reached through the wooden bars and pulled the lever sticking out of the floor beside us.

"Please work," I said.

The ropes really did start moving, pulling the cage, and us with it, swiftly upwards. We clung to the wooden bars. To our horror, the elevator just kept getting faster. I felt sick to my stomach. The ceiling was racing towards us.

"Aren't there any brakes in this thing?" cried Lilli.

Just then the elevator came screeching to a halt from one second to the next, flinging us all into the air a little. We had arrived. Before us lay the exit platform.

In the same instant, the Hat stormed into the room below. He immediately saw us. His gaze moved straight past the eagle and came to rest on the lever that controlled the elevator.

Without a second's hesitation, he ran for it.

"Get out!" I yelled.

We jumped onto the platform beside us. Almost simultaneously, the gangster below pulled the lever and the elevator began whizzing back down.

Before us extended a cavernous tunnel lit up by the dim electrical glow of the occasional lightbulb hanging from the ceiling. It ran in a curve and was so high and wide that a lorry could easily have driven down it. We raced along it.

After a few feet, we came across a heavy, metal door in the wall to our right. We immediately realized where we were: When we'd entered this ancient dungeon, we'd been standing exactly on the other side of the metal door. The ventilation duct we'd abseiled down was there too.

"Here's the exit," I said and pressed a red button by the door handle. To my relief, the door unlocked, and I opened it.

"We have to keep moving! That way to Eckles," said Lilli and pointed down the tunnel.

The bang of the elevator arriving reverberated somewhere behind us.

"The gangster's here," said Marvin wide-eyed.

"Let's go!" I yelled.

Driven by the hope of finding Eckles, we sprinted deeper into the tunnel. Luckily, it continued to run in a curve. This meant that our pursuer couldn't see us, even though he must have already reached the tunnel too by now. He would probably guess we'd escaped through the open metal door. That had to give us a little head start.

"Hey kids!" we suddenly heard Eckles call. His voice didn't come from the puzzle walkie-talkie this time but from an old, wooden door. It had a tiny peephole and was secured with a heavy bolt. We immediately joined forces to pull the bolt aside. When the door sprang open, a man pulled us into his arms and hugged us tight, trembling with excitement and joy.

"I'm so happy to see you. Thank you. Thank you so much," he said, tears in his eyes.

But right at that moment, we heard footsteps again. They were quickly getting closer.

"Hurry. We've got to hide," I said.

We each hid in a different place. Can you find all four hiding places?

No Easy Target

"Shoot," cursed the Hat. "They've set Eckles free. The little wretches!"

The closet door was open a crack, and through it I could see the leader of the gang. I hoped he wouldn't notice the arm of the sweater I'd gotten caught in it while rushing to close it.

We waited till all went quiet, then came out of our hiding places. Lilli had been lying on top of the closet, and Marvin had hidden behind the jackets on the coat rack. James Eckles had been particularly inventive—he'd submerged himself in the full bathtub. To breathe, he'd used a pipe he'd unscrewed from the wall by the bath.

Now we had to hurry. Soon our time would run out, and the elixir would be lost forever. Cautiously but with great determination, we crept outside and reached the bumblebee unseen.

As Marvin put the rotary wings in motion and took off with the usual piercing whirr, the sun was just going down, setting the sky aglow in the prettiest colors.

"There, look!" Eckles yelled. "They're headed for their helicopter."

The Hat and two other gangsters ran across a field towards the helicopter they'd arrived in. Clearly they were going to fly after us.

"Marvin, aren't you an expert at destroying valuable aircraft?" asked Lilli.

"Very funny," he replied and pulled the bumblebee sideways towards the helicopter.

"What do you mean by that? What aircraft?" asked Eckles, who of course didn't know that only hours earlier many of his *flying inventions* had been reduced to rubble thanks to Marvin's first attempt at flying the bumblebee.

"Oh, nothing," murmured Lilli.

Just as the bumblebee was about to crash into the helicopter, Marvin steered it in the opposite direction and increased the thrust. The air pressure threw the helicopter sideways, causing it to topple over and tumble down the hill, shattering the rotor blades. The dented body came to rest at the men's feet. The Hat tore off his jacket and threw it on the ground in a rage. Then he seemed to take a deep breath before sitting down in the grass and staring after us, shaking his head.

That took care of him. And his gang too.

As we flew towards the setting sun, Eckles said, "Look at this. It's a data orb." In his hand he held a marble the size of a fist. "It has to be inserted into the hole at the top of the machine containing the elixir in the Museum of Technology. That will cause the machine to automatically link into the external electricity network, thus ensuring the continued refrigeration of the elixir."

"The Guardians didn't take that data orb away from you?" I asked.

"No. They caught me when I had my bags all packed ready to head for the hills and threw me into the dungeon along with my luggage," explained Eckles. "So there I was, sitting in the dark with my sunscreen and my beach shoes."

A street appeared now, leading into the city. Marvin flew parallel to it, above the fields beside it. A few motorists pointed excitedly at us, and others waved as we sped past.

"How are we going to get to the museum now?" asked Lilli. "You can't fly *into town*, Marvin."

At that moment, we saw the first houses. We were approaching them at an alarming speed.

"This is going to work," murmured Marvin.

Marvin steered the aircraft over the street so we were zooming along only a few feet above the cars driving on it. As we did, each car we flew over caused the bumblebee to rise and every gap between two cars caused it to descend.

"This is going to be the worst grounding in human history," I screamed.

Then we tore into town. Building fronts sped by on either side of us.

"Look out!" cried Lilli as a bus at an intersection moved into our flight path.

"Hold on tight," yelled Eckles and pulled a handle hanging from the ceiling of the cockpit.

In the blink of an eye, the bumblebee was catapulted upwards. *This must be what rocket-assisted takeoff feels like*, I thought. We were briefly able to see over the rooves of the buildings around us before we went screaming into a freefall, only to then speed on at our original altitude again. We were clinging to our seats. And that wasn't about to change for the next few minutes either.

But when we finally reached the Museum of Technology, our time was almost up. Marvin calmly hovered the bumblebee over the square in front of the museum. The building lay before us, dark and impenetrable.

"Only thirty seconds left," said Marvin after a glance at the bumblebee's instruments which showed the exact time.

"Too late, kids," said Eckles woefully.

"The dome," I said. "The machine is right under the glass dome in the roof."

"Take us up, Marvin," said Lilli.

"We'll jump onto the roof," he said and pressed the throttle lever forward. Faster and faster, we raced across the square towards the Museum of Technology. Marvin now held his right hand at the ready on the handle James Eckles had pulled before to catapult us high into the air.

"Now," Marvin yelled.

Instantaneously we shot upwards. At first it looked good. Marvin had initiated the jump at the right moment. We climbed so high, we'd have no trouble landing on the roof of the museum. The glass dome lay right before us as the bumblebee began to freefall again. Then everything went very quickly. Smash! Clang! A hefty shudder ran through the bumblebee. We heard the rotary wings reluctantly come to a standstill.

The bumblebee had landed smack dab in the middle of the glass dome and was stuck fast.

After the initial shock had passed, my gaze fell on the time.

"Twelve seconds," I said.

Marvin opened a window in the cockpit and looked down. On the floor of the museum, directly below us, stood the machine with the elixir. The opening we needed to put the data orb into was on the top of the gadget, gaping expectantly up at us.

"Catch!" yelled Eckles, tossing Marvin the orb.

"Seven seconds," said Marvin, adjusting his glasses and peering downwards. He held the arm with the data orb out in the air, altered the position of his hand a little... and dropped it.

It fell as if in slow motion.

An almost impossible target to hit.

But it looked good. The orb was moving directly towards the opening.

There were still three seconds showing on the machine's digital sign. More than enough time.

But then I noticed something wasn't right. By the time I figured out what, it was already too late.

 What did I see that wasn't right?

The Dungeon

I still recalled quite clearly the life-sized terracotta soldiers on the museum floor. But yesterday, there had been exactly three of them, not four like now. Someone was standing with them. Just as I noticed that, the man moved. He took two quick steps towards the machine and held his hand outstretched above the opening.

The data orb fell into his palm with a slap.

"What?" yelled Marvin.

In the darkness, we could only make out the man's silhouette, but he seemed to look up at us and laugh quietly. At the same time, all the lights on the machine that cooled the elixir went out.

Then the man turned and disappeared.

It took a few moments for us to grasp what had happened. The machine had no power and could no longer refrigerate. The elixir was lost.

"It's all over," Eckles said dejectedly. "The elixir was supposed to be my legacy. My gift to humanity. And instead of helping the world, I've done it a disservice. Now only the Dark Power can produce it. Soon they'll all be able to do anything they want. Their influence will grow beyond measure."

"Who was that?" asked Lilli, furious. "Was that Dr. Sangrey?"

"It was too dark to tell," said Marvin.

"Maybe we'll be able to see when he leaves the museum," she said, pulling herself out the side window of the bumblebee and leaping onto the roof. We followed her example. The next moment, a vehicle sped down the street in front of the museum. It was Dr. Sangrey.

"It's him!" I yelled as the car turned down a side street and disappeared.

"If only we had some evidence against him," said Eckles, "we might have a chance of getting the sale of my inventions to him annulled."

"You'd get your records back, and you could make another batch of the elixir," I yelled excitedly.

"Perhaps," mused Eckles.

"Well, whatever happens, we have to try to bring Dr. Sangrey to justice," said Lilli.

Suddenly the museum's alarm rang out. Dr Sangrey must have shut it off while he was in the building. Just as it had the day before, a heavy metal plate slid across beneath the glass dome, sealing off the exhibit. Screeching loudly, it squashed the bumblebee, which was still stuck in the hole, until its front half was cut off and fell inside the museum with a crash.

"Oh man," moaned Marvin.

"There goes another one," whispered Lilli.

❖ ❖ ❖

Shortly after night fell, the lights of several police cars bathed Dr. Sangrey's country estate in a flickering blue. James Eckles's declaration that he'd been kidnapped by Dr. Sangrey had convinced Inspector Hallewell to look into the matter again after all. She even agreed to take us along since as eyewitnesses we might be able to catch Dr. Sangrey out in any lies he might tell. James Eckles needed a rest and decided not to come.

Lilli, Marvin and I now stood with Inspector Hallewell across from Dr. Sangrey once more. I could yet again feel the piercing glare coming from his black eye sockets. We had already confronted him with all our accusations, leaving nothing out.

Dr. Sangrey let it all sink in a moment then took a deep breath and cleared his throat. "Let me reassure you, Inspector," he replied. "None of it is true."

I had actually been expecting some kind of nasty insult, but Dr. Sangrey was too cunning for that.

"First," he began, "I didn't know a thing about this treasure hunt until just now. And you didn't mention it at all this afternoon. Such an unusual newspaper ad has never crossed my desk.

"Second, I may have been at Bloodhound Castle on the evening in question, but I didn't do anything wrong. I did, however, manage to injure my right foot there.

"Third, I have had no contact with any criminals. I never hired a gang to break into the Sphere and steal or destroy something.

"Fourth, I didn't sneak into the museum to sabotage the attempted rescue of some kind of elixir. I wouldn't even know how to switch off the alarm system to break in.

"Finally, I haven't left this office since you visited me here this afternoon." An evil glint appeared in his dark eye sockets. "Who are you going to believe, Inspector? A few random kids or me?" Now he turned to us and said, "So close the door behind you again, kids, because there's no reason to doubt my testimony."

Marvin, however, started clapping his hands and bobbing up and down excitedly. "I know a reason," he said quietly.

"I noticed something about your testimony too," I said.

"He's lying, Inspector," said Lilli, "and we can prove it."

How many of Dr. Sangrey's assertions can you refute or cast doubt on and how?

One   Two to three   Four   All five (nearly impossible)

The Beginning of the End

After we put our heads together a few moments to discuss our observations, Lilli let Dr. Sangrey have it.

"Well, first, your *right* foot isn't hurt at all. We saw you through the window of the cottage near Bloodhound Castle. You had your *left* foot elevated then and were pretending you'd hurt it. Marvin did a sketch of you then that can prove it," said Lilli.

"I even have it with me," said Marvin, holding up his sketch pad.

"Nonsense," said Dr. Sangrey. "Then you just drew it wrong." You could hear a certain hostility in his voice now after all.

"Second," Lilli went on, "you certainly have seen the newspaper ad about the treasure hunt before. When we visited you the first time, it was lying on your desk. You'd made handwritten notes on it. Now it's here, in the wastepaper basket."

"That doesn't prove anything. I read the newspaper daily, but I never look at the ads," he said.

Careful not to get too close to Dr. Sangrey, I walked over to the wastepaper basket, pulled the newspaper out and unfolded it. Beside the treasure hunt ad were scrawled the words '*James Eckles?*'.

"Certainly looks like you've seen it before," I said.

"That's not my handwriting. No idea who wrote that," he yelled furiously.

"Our experts will easily be able to determine whether it's your handwriting or not," said Inspector Hallewell calmly but firmly.

"Third, you certainly have had contact with the gang that, among other things, broke into the Sphere," said Lilli. "Part of the gang's mission there was to steal a valuable binder labelled *Inventions: Sphere Laboratory*. It was a blue binder, and on the spine it had a yellow circle with a red circle in the middle. And now, by some miracle, that binder is here in your drawer."

"There are lots of those binders," Dr. Sangrey said.

"I touched the binder in the Sphere," I told Inspector Hallewell. "You just have to check if my fingerprints are on it."

The inspector gave me a smile and nodded appreciatively. "Then we'll be able to prove unequivocally whether or not it's the binder in question. If it is, then your connection to the gang is established. By the way, we're taking them into custody as we speak. They were walking back into town after their helicopter was *somehow* destroyed."

"Fourth," went on Marvin this time, "you certainly do know how to switch the alarm system in the museum on and off. It can only be done with a special keycard—Mr. Baker from security showed us his. A card just like it is hanging there next to your keyboard."

"Enough! I've had it up to here with you kids. Who do you think you are?" Dr. Sangrey raged.

"Finally," said the inspector, raising her voice in warning, "you just incriminated yourself when you claimed not to have left this office since our visit this afternoon. Why are you wearing outdoor shoes? You were wearing comfortable slippers before. Surely they'd be better for a supposedly injured foot?"

Dr. Sangrey stared at the inspector, stunned. He was at a loss for words.

"You're under arrest," said Inspector Hallewell and pressed a button on her walkie-talkie, at which four more agents entered the office. They quickly ran up the stairs to join us.

"How can this be?" asked Dr. Sangrey, incredulous. "A few kids outsmarted me?"

Handcuffs clicked onto his wrists. The police officers pulled him to his feet, and as he was led past us, he leaned down and whispered, "You've dealt our organization a great blow today. The Guardian Supreme won't be happy."

It was the first time we'd seen Dr. Sangrey up close. A shiver ran down my spine. His eyes really were black, as was his mouth.

Then he straightened again and strode down the steps without the slightest limp.

"Don't worry, kids," said the inspector. "Thanks to the information you've uncovered, the police will be able to initiate an investigation into Dr. Sangrey's organization, effective immediately. I promise you, today is the beginning of the end for the Guardians of the Dark Power."

As Dr. Sangrey and the officers accompanying him were about to leave the office one floor down, Lilli called out, "Dr. Sangrey? Be a dear and close the door behind you, hmm?"

He stared back at us. His black mouth twisted into a smile. He seemed to like her sass. Then the officers led him out of the room.

Instantaneously, a huge weight fell from my shoulders. We'd proven him guilty. He was probably a real bigshot in the Guardians' ranks. Maybe the police would even manage to convict the rest of the members of the secret order. But I doubted it. If the elixir really were as powerful as James Eckles had described and the Guardians of the Dark Power used it for their own benefit, they'd be practically unstoppable.

I took a long drag on my asthma inhaler.

"Good triumphed over evil," said Marvin, clapping his hands and bobbing happily up and down.

"It did today, anyway," I said with a smile.

"Yeah, and as for tomorrow, we'll be there too," said Lilli, grinning and shrugging her shoulders.

"I think I'll put your names forward for a certificate of honor," said the inspector. "And you'll definitely be on the news."

I looked at Lilli and Marvin and knew exactly what they were thinking. "To be honest, we'd prefer to stay out of the limelight," I said.

The inspector gave us a look of surprise. "Well, I'll do my best," she replied. "But a certificate of honor would be alright?"

"A certificate of honor would be awesome," I said. My two best friends and I were relieved our adventure had ended so well. We'd had a lot of luck. But secretly, I was already dying to go on our next one.

THE END

Psst. Something new is coming. Turn the page.

SOMETHING
NEW IS
COMING
CHRISTMAS
2020

TO THE
ADVENTURERS
AND DETECTIVES
CLUB.
LET THE TRUTH
BE KNOWN

Check out the all new series:
Young Reader Mini Mysteries

- **Picture Mysteries**
- **Fascinating Facts**
- **Tips for Adventurers and Detectives**

For readers aged 6 and up!

HINTS

The chapter hints are listed in reverse order, to avoid spoilers when you read them using a small mirror.

First assertion: In chapter twenty-two we already found an object here. You'll find this claim is a lie, if it's a lie, it tells us this claim is a lie... in the last chapter too.

Second assertion: Go back to chapter fifteen and check his claim. In that chapter, he told Digby he had injured his arm... was therefore keeping it elevated.

Third assertion: What was the gang supposed to steal from the Shayfe before activating the self-destruct sequence? How was it described in chapter sixteen?

Fourth assertion: What did the museum guard tell us about the alarm system in chapter three? Once you've retraced your memory, have one more close look at the picture in the last chapter.

Fifth assertion: What might indicate that Dr. Sangley had left his office since our heroes visited it last that two? Look at his clothing.

Chapter 30

To solve this puzzle, you'll have to go back almost to the beginning of the story. Have another look at the picture in chapter
two.

Chapter 29

To find Timmi and Lilli, look closely at the closet. What has
changed? As for Marvin, he has hidden standing up. And our
inventor was very resourceful when finding a place to lie low.

Chapter 28

The riddle asks you to look at things from an unusual point
of view. This can be taken literally. Look at the ceiling or
the door from below or from the light at a very sharp angle.
As sharp as it you were about to bite into your book (or your
reader).

Chapter 27

Here, only those who can take some distance when looking
at life's challenges are supposed to get past. So move away
from the picture and watch as the blurry black symbols in the
background get clearer, and clearer. Then you'll see the correct
code.

Chapter 26

The riddle tells you to turn your perspective upside down.
Take it literally by turning the book upside down.

Chapter 25

Three of the four grids aren't that easy to see at first. The
first of the three you'll find it if you look at what the grass by
the campfire is doing. The second you'll find by paying attention to differences in color. The third and final, color.
Find what lies in the distance by examining what lies in the distance.

Chapter 24

Only one of the pictured objects actually 'hates, touching
water.

Chapter 16

Grab a pencil and draw a path to the farthest box you can reach before you would have to cross a motion detector. Then look at what changes under the next phase and extend your line. Keep switching back and forth between the two phases and extending the line until you make it to the private area. The doors are all open and you can safely walk through the rooms. Timmi found a path that led him along the right-hand side to start with.

Chapter 17

If you look in a mirror, what is on the left will be on the right and vice versa. Try it.

Chapter 18

At first the chalice is empty. But how many coins does it take to change that? So how many coins will fit into an empty chalice?

Chapter 19

There are certain things you just never want to read.

Chapter 20

What do we know about Dr. Sangrey? Look in chapter fourteen.

Chapter 21

Whatever has Timmi concerned, it can only be seen indirectly.

Chapter 22

Have another good look at the picture in chapter twenty. Something from that picture reappears here in chapter twenty-two.

Chapter 23

The M on the treasure map has a specific shape. You'll be able to find the same shape in three places on the picture (but not on the city map).

Use a mirror to read!

Chapter 15

To find the answer, you'll have to take a good look at the picture from chapter fourteen too.

Chapter 14

Martin realizes the dogs, even aren't really growing, but it's something else that's making it seem like they are. But what exactly is it that is growing? Search the surrounding area to find the solution.

Chapter 14 — BONUS QUESTION

How could paintbrushes be faked? Can you find anything that could have been used to do it?

Chapter 13

In the text, we learned about the buttons and what happened when you press them. Sometimes the solution is right in front of your face.

Chapter 12

The threads are so tangled up in one another that there's no way to accurately tell which one goes where. There must be another way to solve the puzzle.

Chapter 11

There are lots of symbols in this room, but only the one we're looking for is shaped like the W on the edge of the puzzle piece on the treasure map. It's not even very small.

Chapter 10

In the museum, the Hat was in disguise. But he has an unmistakable distinguishing feature which you can see in chapter three.

Chapter 10 — BONUS QUESTION

What information about how the police operate did our heroes obtain in chapter seven? A key detail mentioned in chapter seven can be found in the picture for chapter ten.

Chapter 9

You need to use a couple of objects together. You need a thin stick and the towel from the radiator. What could you do with them?

Chapter 8

Our heroes' combined weight is causing a telltale difference between the top and bottom pictures.

Chapter 7

The security cameras didn't get any shots of the Hat's face. But isn't there another camera which might have gotten a picture of him?

Chapter 6

Some of the drawings lying around look a bit like maps. But only the map our heroes are looking for is clearly labelled "Street Map".

Chapter 5

What do we know about the man with the hat? Using your knowledge, can you figure out which footprints belong to him?

Chapter 4

The man with the hat has gotten changed. He has turned his hat and his jacket inside out so that you now see the color of the lining. Can you make out the color of the lining in the picture in chapter three? If not, don't worry. Just look for the person carrying the polka-dot bag.

Chapter 3

One of the people has an item with them in Marvin's sketch that is now somewhere else.

Chapter 2

An object that was still present in the top picture is missing in the bottom picture.

Chapter 1

Timmi had been reading before Lilli came to visit. Is there a way you can tell how long he'd been doing that already?

ACKNOWLEDGEMENTS

It took a full year to develop this book and I would like to thank everyone who stood by my side - but first and foremost my wife Anja who cared for our little Emmelie and made it possible for me to actually get this done. Kisses!

❖ ❖ ❖

I would also like to thank those who have read this book throughout its various development stages – namely (in alphabetic order):

Dr. Markus Bruckner
Dr. Nicolas David
Albrecht Denzer
Martina Denzer
Sascha Gemming
Anja Wagner
Marie Wagner

❖ ❖ ❖

Thank you to Javi and Tracy for delivering outstanding work, even in the face of challenging deadlines. You guys rock.

❖ ❖ ❖

As always, special thanks go to my mom for being the best mom in the world and to my dad for telling me to do what makes me happy.

FUN FACTS

This book contains a puzzle that is unrelated to the story and involves all thirty-one main illustrations. A hint can be found on the cover. Go to www.timmitobbson.com if you think you have the solution.

❖ ❖ ❖

Some of the objects displayed in the backgrounds of various illustrations (such as in chapter twenty-four) are inspired by movies.

❖ ❖ ❖

The walk on the abandoned railway was inspired by *Stand by Me*.

❖ ❖ ❖

The hounds of Blackhound Manor were inspired by *Sherlock Holmes*.

❖ ❖ ❖

The inventor was originally called James Edison. That name was dismissed since some found the similarity to real-life inventor Thomas Edison confusing.

❖ ❖ ❖

The sign on Timmi's bedroom door reads *A&D - Access for Club Members Only*. A&D stands for Adventurers and Detectives. This club plays a major role in the new Timmi Tobbson mini mysteries series, aimed at readers aged 6 and up, scheduled to release in late 2020/early 2021.

ABOUT THE AUTHOR

Jens I. Wagner lives with his beloved wife, his daughter Emmelie Amilia, and two big, orange cats right at the edge of a forest near Frankfurt, Germany.

He earned a master's degree at Oxford University where he loved being part of the Christ Church College community.

Jens is a fan of all kinds of fiction ranging from *Indiana Jones* to *James Bond.*

Do you like this book and want to help spread the word?

At the time of writing, we have no big publishing house to support us and it is you, and only you, who can make all the difference. Here is how you can help:

1. You can go to timmitobbson.com and register as a fan. That way I can keep in touch with you, share exciting news, ask for your opinion and give you a glimpse behind the scenes.

2. Leave a review on the internet platform of your choice. Every review helps us gain visibility, increasing the chances of us extending the series. Reviews are super important.

3. Tell your friends, teachers, bookstore, library, book club, etc. about Timmi Tobbson. Every bookstore and library should know about and stock this book.

Should your school, book club or any other group order ten or more copies, go ahead and write to me (at timmi@timmitobbson. com). Let me know how many copies were ordered, and I will send you just as many book plates (stickers that go inside the book) with my real (not printed) signature on them!

Whichever way you choose to help: Thank you so much!

All the best,

J. I. Wagner